SIREN
Publishing

Ménage Everlasting

CW01521752

MADE MEN 8:
ALL OR NOTHING
DIXIE LYNN DWYER

Made Men 8: All or Nothing

Alda wants to be more than just a one-night-stand, but fighting an attraction to four badass made men might prove to be deadly. She tries to resist their charms and their lack of communication because they're so tough, commanding, and have reputations to keep. But when they turn her away after a night of bliss, she's pissed, believes she deserves more, and looks elsewhere.

Their connection is powerful, but other factors affect her judgment—like the two other sexy, wealthy business men who respect her and pay attention, a business deal in her favor, and choices that become a game of trusting her heart or her gut, of choosing passion or turning away for something more suitable and safe.

When Royce, Brew, Train, and Logic challenge her to take all or nothing, the risk could end not only her career but also her life.

Genre: Contemporary, Ménage a Trois/Quatre, Romantic Suspense
Length: 64,822 words

MADE MEN 8: ALL OR NOTHING

Dixie Lynn Dwyer

Siren Publishing, Inc.
www.SirenPublishing.com

A SIREN PUBLISHING BOOK

MADE MEN 8: ALL OR NOTHING
Copyright © 2017 by Dixie Lynn Dwyer

ISBN: 978-1-64010-860-8

First Publication: October 2017

Cover design by Les Byerley
All art and logo copyright © 2017 by Siren Publishing, Inc.

PUBLISHER
Siren Publishing, Inc.
www.SirenPublishing.com

DEDICATION

Dear readers, thank you for purchasing this legal copy of *All or Nothing*. Alda is a very strong, professional woman, and hanging around her girlfriends and their love interests have surely taught her a thing or two about made men.

So when Alda starts having this strong attraction to Brew, Royce, Logic, and Train, she puts on the breaks, slams up the walls, and questions the power of their connection and attraction.

Those made men aren't exactly ready to admit how Alda makes them feel, and the idea of being vulnerable and weak isn't something they are used to or willing to admit to.

That denial sends her straight into danger all because they couldn't accept reality or fate itself. May you enjoy their story as they learn that in a relationship like this one, and an attraction so strong, they must give all or nothing, or lose her completely.

Happy reading,
HUGS!

Dixie

ABOUT THE AUTHOR

People seem to be more interested in my name than where I get my ideas for my stories from. So I might as well share the story behind my name with all my readers.

My momma was born and raised in New Orleans. At the age of twenty, she met and fell in love with an Irishman named Patrick Riley Dwyer. Needless to say, the family was a bit taken aback by this as they hoped she would marry a family friend. It was a modern day arranged marriage kind of thing and my momma downright refused.

Being that my momma's families were descendants of the original English speaking Southerners, they wanted the family blood line to stay pure. They were wealthy and my father's family was poor.

Despite attempts by my grandpapa to make Patrick leave and destroy the love between them, my parents married. They recently celebrated their sixtieth wedding anniversary.

I am one of six children born to Patrick and Lynn Dwyer. I am a combination of both Irish and a true Southern belle. With a name like Dixie Lynn Dwyer it's no wonder why people are curious about my name.

Just as my parents had a love story of their own, I grew up intrigued by the lifestyles of others. My imagination as well as my need to stray from the straight and narrow made me into the woman I am today.

Enjoy *All or Nothing* and allow your imagination to soar freely.

For all titles by Dixie Lynn Dwyer, please visit
www.bookstrand.com/dixie-lynn-dwyer

MADE MEN 8: ALL OR NOTHING

DIXIE LYNN DWYER

Prologue

"Which one?" Matt asked his partner.

"The redhead," Shady replied and chewed on the toothpick as he watched the women by the bar.

"Are you sure? I was thinking the brunette looks easier," Matt said and then looked around them, making sure that no one was watching, or could be suspicious. The club was crowded enough and the redhead was with several other women and all flirting, drinking heavily, making them all easy targets.

"Nah, the redhead is what the boss will like," Shady added and then ordered two more drinks.

Matt thought about that. Their boss had particular tastes. This redhead had a bit more muscle on her but a super body. The boss did say to change it up a little and choose something a little different. A redhead would fit that criteria as well as her designer style. The boss was antsy when he was traveling, and would be in the penthouse within the next hour. They needed to move quickly and have her ready for him.

"Let's do this," Matt said to Shady and both men made their way over to the ladies.

* * * *

Cindy was laughing at something Beth was saying. These two super hot guys that came over to flirt and then some others guys did, too, and they were all dancing and having a good time. She could feel her head getting a little fuzzy when Colby, the one guy who she noticed watching her from the bar with his friend earlier, offered her a drink. She had half of it and now she felt really buzzed.

He wrapped an arm around her waist and led her off the dance floor.

"Maybe you overdid it out there, honey," he said and she smiled and nodded.

"I guess so. It is pretty crowded," she replied, her gut clenched, and then the room began to spin. The music started to really slow down and she held on to Colby tighter.

"Maybe she needs fresh air. It's so damn hot and crowded in the place and the music is loud," Lance, the other guy, said, raising his voice over the music, which to her sounded distorted, and Colby agreed.

"Come on, Cindy. We'll take care of you," Colby told her and they headed through the crowd, her legs starting to feel weak. It felt like Colby was practically lifting her along the way, and out the back door. The cool evening air hit her skin. The sound of traffic, cars honking and the smell of food from vending trucks attacked her senses. She felt like she was getting worse.

She gripped on to Colby. She stared into his dark brown eyes. They were narrowed at her and a smirk showed on his face. She hoped she wasn't embarrassing herself.

"I think something is wrong. I didn't drink that much, but I…feel wasted." She slurred her speech and he guided her down the sidewalk and to the corner street along with Lance.

"I think you sound perfect, and just about ready."

"Ready for what?" she asked.

"Your date with Tatum," Lance said and Colby helped her get into the backseat of an SUV. She inhaled the smell of men's cologne, leather seats, and lavender.

Colby held her on his lap as Lance disappeared. Then she felt the SUV moving.

Suddenly Cindy couldn't move. Her arms went limp. All muscle control failed and she heard Colby's muffled voice.

"She has got a great set of breasts. The boss is going to enjoy her."

"Yes, he will, and look at the time. He'll be there within the hour."

"So we can explore her a little, too. To get her ready," Colby said and smiled down at her and then began to undo her top. Suddenly there were three of them. His face multiplied, her head spun, and then darkness overtook her vision.

Chapter 1

The soft sounds of Italian music added to the ambiance of "Oliva," the name of the martini bar Alda, Donata, and Alessa were starting the evening at. Donata and Alessa were talking to two guys they knew who worked for Tudoro Garlitto, Mickey, and Spence. She was thinking about work as she sipped at her pomegranate martini and took in the atmosphere of the place. The low lighting, the upscale décor, and the Tuscany and industrial influence around the place. It wasn't too big. She knew there was more intimate seating in the back room along with a fireplace that was always packed in the winter months. She liked the bar area the most with the old-fashioned brass and cherrywood bar, the mirrored backdrop and lots of original wood work from centuries ago. She was pretty sure this place had a lot of history.

"Need another one, sweetheart?" the bartender asked her and she shook her head.

"The boss is buying," he told her and the bartender nodded behind her. She turned to look and there was Logic Foster, one of the Coglonie brothers' security guys. She felt her heart race and warmth hit her cheeks at the sight of him. Six feet three, wide shoulders, blond hair and those eyes. Jesus, he had killer eyes and looking at him made her body react big time. Not smart.

Her mind processed what the bartender had said. *The boss is buying.* Did that mean Logic owned the place or the Coglonies? She knew the Coglonies owned many places around New York.

"Good evening, Alda," he said softly to her, yet that deep voice still seemed to penetrate her skin on an intimate level.

"Hi, Logic. How are you?" she asked, sliding off the stool to greet him out of respect one gives to a man of his power and authority in the organized crime world. His hands went right to her hips, then one slid up her back. She felt a mix of emotions as women looked on, admiring his ass for sure, and then sending daggers her way. She felt self-conscious. She definitely didn't like feeling on display and she stiffened a moment as he pressed closer, looked her over, and gave her a wink.

His cologne attacked her senses. His manliness, and the feel of hard muscles and large, warm hands connected with her body.

"Doing well. What are you doing here?" he asked, and kissed her cheek, wrapped his arm around her waist and pressed close to her. She inhaled, shocked by the sensations she felt and by his move. The last few times she bumped into him or spent time with him and Train, they were flirty, but held back, and were even called away for some sort of "business" with the Coglonie men. She wondered how Giada handled her men and their business positions. Logic made her very nervous.

When he released her she instantly felt the loss, which was so odd. Plenty of times men hugged her, maybe took advantage of pressing up close to her and she felt nothing. Logic, on the other hand, made her heart race and her feel like she needed to impress him or something. It was so weird. Did she think she wasn't good enough for him? Maybe it was all the attention he, Train, Royce, and Brew got. Why she pooled them all together she didn't know, but she did. She saw them as one unit.

He slid his hand at her lower back and looked at the bartender. "She'll take another one and I'll have Captain and Coke," he told the bartender.

She eased back onto the stool and crossed her legs. He stood with his back against the bar and looked at her.

"Thank you for the drink. It wasn't necessary."

"I saw you immediately and hoped to buy you a drink. Maybe talk alone," he said, holding her gaze but sweeping his eyes over her chest. The dress she wore accentuated her full breasts, yet wasn't too sexy at all. The bartender put the drinks down and he passed her the pomegranate martini. She couldn't believe what he was saying. Now her nervous meter went up another notch.

"What shall we toast to?" he asked her, holding her gaze. Those deep blue eyes, blond hair, and the tight dress shirt in blue he wore showed off his muscles and those incredible eyes.

"Martinis!" Donata chimed in and Alessa, Mickey, and Spence laughed.

Logic looked back at Alda as if the interruption annoyed him. His dark blue eyes narrowed, and she could just imagine what a man like him looked like pissed off. She did recall how demanding Royce, Brew, Train, and Logic were when Giada went missing. Royce and Logic had placed guards on Alda as a precaution, which was something that happened before when one of her other friends was in danger. It was the looks in their eyes, the cold, hard expressions, and their commanding orders that interested her. She thought they were flirting several times, and even touched her, caressed her arm, hell, when each of them greeted her hello she always felt a light caress across her ass but it was so quick, so light she wondered if she imagined it. Perhaps she just wanted to experience what her friends were experiencing. The attention, the care and protection of made men. Or simply a ménage?

"To martinis," he said and they clinked glasses. As they took sips they both held one another's gazes. Something was brewing here and she wondered what?

* * * *

Logic took this opportunity to enjoy Alda's company. She was gorgeous, classy, professional, and totally out of his league. A woman as gorgeous, sexy, and professional would want nothing to do with a made man, an enforcer for made men like the Coglonies. Although he, Train, Brew, and Royce owned their own businesses with the bosses, and established their own monies and successes, it was done secretively. Their position as enforcers for Dominick, Giuseppe, and Andreas Coglonie was top priority. Things were changing though. More men, members of the Coglonie family, were taking over security as Dominick and the crew made changes. Their first priority was Giada. He envied them.

He stared at Alda. Her thick, gorgeous brown hair a little past her shoulders was done up in large curls. He loved when she straightened it, too, and it swayed behind her sexy, muscular back. The woman had one hell of a body, and the last time he saw her at Club X, she wore a low dip dress that accentuated her large breasts and revealed a little too much skin. He nearly clocked a guy who had been hitting on her and stroking her bare shoulder. He wondered if she was disappointed that the guy never returned to hit on her after he went to the men's room? Logic got rid of him quickly, threatening him to stay clear of Alda or else.

He felt a bit dickish. There he was, staking some sort of claim or authority over the woman and she wasn't his woman. Oh, but he would love for her to be. He just wasn't the commitment kind of guy, nor were his buddies Brew, Royce, and Train. They were one more fucked up than the other.

"So, what are you doing here, Logic? The bartender referred to you as the boss?" she asked him and took another sip of her martini.

Some guy came over to order drinks and Logic took the opportunity to move closer to her. He placed a hand on the back of her chair and stroked her bare arm. Tonight she wore a simple black dress that hugged her figure. She looked sexy. He licked his lips and stared at her lips. She swallowed hard. Damn, she was feeling the attraction, too.

"Train and I run the place. For the Coglonies," he added as she looked around as if searching for Train. Could she be interested in him, too? Fuck, they all talked about her. Except Royce. He remained straight-faced and all business. With any other woman Logic could do that, too. Hell, he could screw a woman and get what he wanted from her and then never talk to her again. Alda was different. Alda affected him and he didn't even kiss her yet. He practically feared getting that close, yet here he was flirting, touching, looking for maybe a little taste just to get this curiosity out of his head.

"That's great. I didn't even know that they owned the place. I remember Giada saying that the Coglonies own multiple bars and restaurants. Do you both help out with them, too?" she asked.

Someone bumped into her chair as the bar area got more and more crowded. He gave the guy a mean expression and then he felt the hand on his hand. He looked down at Alda.

"It's okay," she said and eased off the bar stool and then stepped right next to the bar.

When she released his hand, the sensations still affecting his entire body, he slid his palm along her waist and pulled her close to him.

"Maybe you should stay closer. That guy nearly elbowed you in the head," he said, staring at her lips. They were parted, her green eyes wide as if shocked by his move or maybe the feel of him so close. He pushed the connection a little further and maneuvered her so his palm was half over her lower back and ass. Fuck, she had a superb ass. It stuck out all sexy and curvy. She didn't pull away but brought her martini to her lips and took a long sip, like she needed it to steady her. He felt as if no amount of shots of alcohol in the world could numb what he was feeling right now. Possessive, lustful, needy, and it didn't help that she looked at him with the same expression. He needed to slow down or he would do something stupid. Like kiss her. She wasn't some slut, or a woman who slept around. His curiosity about her made him dig a little. Not too much like some stalker, but enough to know she wasn't easy, and she was a professional woman.

"I've never seen you here with your friends. Have you hung out here before?" he asked her, still holding her and she was still allowing it.

"Only twice. Donata and Alessa like the clubs and dancing."

He slid his palm up and down her back and then over her ass to her hip, then back again.

"How about you? You like to dance?"

"Sometimes, but it gets a little crazy and people annoy me," she said to him.

He squinted his eyes at her. "What do you mean?"

"Men. They think they can just touch you when they want to, or like you're fair game because you're at a club, a bar and having fun."

He eased his hand away from her, wondering if she was telling him he was being like that.

She pressed closer and grabbed his arm.

"I didn't mean you, Logic. You asked about the clubs and dancing," she said to him and then she looked flushed, like she was embarrassed, sort of admitting she was liking him touching her. Well, hell, he was liking it, too. He slid his hand back over her hip and then to her lower back and ass. He pulled her close, leaned down, and whispered next to her ear.

"I'm glad you don't mind me touching you." He pressed his lips to her neck, inhaled her perfume and felt his cock grow thick and hard. Her intake of breath indicated she felt his reaction to her and he didn't mind her knowing what she did to him. Perhaps it would lead her to accepting whatever they could share. Even just a night.

When she pulled back and downed the rest of her martini and looked toward her friends, he realized what they both must have felt scared her. She was putting on the brakes.

He pulled her back and leaned nonchalantly against the bar.

"So, how is work going? Any new projects or anything?" he asked.

She squinted at him.

"You know where I work and what I do?"

He was quick. Always had been.

"Of course. The ladies and the guys talk. I heard it's a small upcoming company with great products. A guy's name, right?" he asked. She nodded.

"MAX. It's a great little company. I've been with them for the last couple of years and hoping that as they transition to international sales, which is what the owners are after, that I won't be forced to look for another job."

He squinted at her. "Why would you have to look for another job if you help them to achieve that status?" he asked.

"Well, I've worked for several other companies through college and afterward, and each time the companies begin to expand and succeed there's a buyout. I've had three severance packages since graduating college and working in this profession. That's insane."

"Good severance packages or not really because of the short periods of time?" he asked.

"Actually, very good packages, which gave me time to search for jobs I felt fit me best. It's worked out so far, but times are changing. It isn't so easy to find a job in my field."

"What exactly is your title?" he asked, although he already knew and he was quite impressed.

"Assistant sales manager and creative marketing assistant. Basically two separate jobs in one."

"Why is that? Seems like a job for more than one person."

"Oh, it is. But the company was small when we started and I think Maxwell and Haley, the owners, are so used to me doing both jobs and successfully that they never hired on more people. If they go internationally, and the product lines continue to expand, they won't have a choice. I would go insane. I mean, I'm going crazy right now because the two people in charge of coming up with a design for these new products aren't doing well at it. The bosses are annoyed and I'm overworked as is with other aspects of the business. It's a stressful mess," she said and he reached out and stroked her jaw. She stared up at him and he gave her a small smile.

"I bet you're really good at your job. That you'll figure out a way to resolve the problems and come out on top," he said. She licked her lower lip and fuck, he wanted to taste her. He started to lower down, gauging whether she would let him or not and then Donata interrupted right before his lips touched hers.

"Hey, you just about ready to go to Club X?"

He felt Alda press her hand to his hip and squeeze like she was annoyed at the interruption. Now that his head cleared a moment he processed what almost happened. If he kissed her, he would want more. More would mean conflict because men in their positions couldn't date anyone. Like their bosses, they had enemies, people who would want to hurt anyone close to them. Remaining unaffected by anyone and anything gave them an imaginary power over their enemies. When a man showed weakness to one woman consistently then that weakness was a target. One men in their position, in his position, couldn't afford.

He stepped back.

"Well, it was good seeing you, Alda. You ladies enjoy the club scene," he said and she narrowed her eyes at him and then her cheeks looked red.

"Come on, sexy woman, I heard there are a bunch of hot guys at Club X and even that one guy who has had his eyes on you. See you around, Logic," Donata said and linked her arm through Alda's, who looked embarrassed by Donata's comment.

So some guy was hitting on her and had his eyes on her? Who the fuck was he? He watched them leave and Alda glanced over her shoulder at him and he couldn't help the jealous scowl on his face. As they disappeared through the crowd he called Brew.

* * * *

"Why did you say that in front of Logic?" Alda reprimanded Donata and Donata laughed. Alessa hailed a cab.

"To make Logic jealous, of course. He doesn't need to know that the guy who has been eyeing you is one of his team members, Brew. Those guys need to make a move already. You've been drooling over them for months and they keep their distance," Donata said and the cab stopped and they got inside.

"I think they're not the dating kind. You know, the whole enforcers thing and stuff. They get called into action at all hours of the night and day for different things and they are all pissed off all the time and maybe need to be to show no fears or weakness," Alessa said to them.

"Look at you analyzing the enforcers in the circle. Is that why you think Lenox, Cobra, Roman, and Ziek haven't made a move on you?" Donata asked Alessa.

"I don't know, maybe it's the same reason why Turbo and his buddies haven't made a move on you, Donata, or it could be your pretend party girl ways stopping them," Alessa said and Donata's mouth gaped open.

Alessa laughed.

"I know you have the hots for them, Donata, so stop teasing Alda and me. Instead of getting frustrated we should be planning some sort of strategic attack."

"Well, I was doing that for Alda."

"You didn't need to, Donata, I think Logic was going to kiss me."

"Right there by the bar and after one drink? Do I have to teach you everything, girl? You need to make them want it, and crave it, beg for it, and get them in the palm of your hands," Donata stated.

"No, I wanted him to kiss me. The attraction is there and each time we talk it gets stronger."

"Talk?" Donata stated and exhaled.

"Yes, talk. If I can't talk to them, have a simple conversation and feel like they're paying attention, then surely I'm not going to be intimate with them."

"You are out of your mind. Maybe the sex, the lust is what will draw them in and keep them wanting more," Donata said.

"There you go, all talk again. You don't want to get used just like Alessa and I don't want to. Plus, our good friends are all involved with men associated with the men we're attracted to. If things don't work out, it will surely put some distance between our girlfriends and us. I don't want that to happen."

"Well, Alda, if you let Logic kiss you, what do you think would have happened?" Alessa asked her.

"I don't know, but I have a feeling life just wouldn't be the same anymore, and truthfully, I just don't know if that's what I want right now or at all," Alda said to them.

She also thought about her cousins C.J. and Randy. They hung out with these two guys, Brendan and Fogerty, who were trouble. When Alda spoke to C.J. and Randy about getting away from Brendan and Fogerty, they both got pissed and asked her to hook them up with one of her friends' boyfriends to work for organized crime. Seriously? She wasn't even dating a guy connected but she was getting hit up for introductions for job interviews? It annoyed her, just like C.J. and Randy's attitudes and the way they looked for trouble. Uncle Carter and Aunt Lilly didn't need the constant aggravation.

The cab stopped and they arrived at Club X. Alda wasn't quite in the mood now, but her friends were and she wouldn't be the one to end the night so soon.

* * * *

"So what do you want me to do about it?" Brew asked Logic over the phone.

"See who the fucking guy is and get rid of him."

"What?" Brew asked, shocked at Logic for even calling him and asking him to do this.

"I thought we discussed her and being off limits," Brew said to him.

"Something happened tonight," Logic stated.

Brew exhaled.

"What the fuck happened?" Brew asked then took a sip from his drink and looked around the club. Train stood beside him and Royce was talking with Giada and Dominick by the bar.

"I'll tell you about it later. I'm stuck here for the night," Logic said to him.

"I'm not going to get involved with this. You want to screw around and risk pissing off Giada and the bosses then so be it. I got a lot of shit going on here. Three assholes already attempted to push their way into the private area, I've got one sick bartender about to pass out, and several small groups of guys getting rowdy. I can't be worrying about your lust interest," Brew said to Logic.

"Say that to me later on and after you see her tonight and talk to her."

"I'm not talking to her," Brew replied and now grabbed Train's attention.

"Sure you won't. Denying it is getting harder and harder. I need to go. Just watch out for her," Logic said and ended the call.

Brew exhaled and placed the phone back on his hip under his dress jacket.

"What was that all about?" Train asked him.

"Alda," Brew said and narrowed his eyes. Just the thought of her got him uncomfortable, and put him on edge. He needed to deny the attraction to her. It wouldn't be smart to get involved with their bosses' woman's friend. Besides, their schedules and lifestyles left no room for commitment with a chick. He for one didn't need the aggravation or the extra burden of having one woman. He liked his life. He liked not having some woman clinging to him and asking for dates and shit. He liked easy lays, one-night stands when he needed to find release, and knocking people around. He, Train, Logic, and Royce were enforcers, business partners for the Coglonie family. Though things were changing and they were taking bigger responsibilities of the businesses, it didn't mean they were settling down.

They sure didn't need some high maintenance bombshell of a woman like Alda messing with their fucking heads. It was bad enough that the sight of her alone gave him a hard on.

"Why is Logic talking about Alda?" Train asked him.

"I don't know what the fuck he was rambling on about. Seeing her at Oliva, something happened and now he wants me to make sure some guy doesn't hit on her or something."

"Some guy is messing with her?" Train asked and sat up from the bar stool.

"Whoa, hold on, killer, I didn't say that, and neither did Logic. He just said something happened and it sounds like he wants her in his bed."

"What the fuck? He can't do that to her. She's sweet, not some whore. Plus she's Giada's friend. Giada will have his ass."

"We've been over this. We'll find out exactly what happened later on. Let's just keep our heads out of our asses, please," Brew said and then flexed his arms. He sure didn't need any drama in his life. Women brought on drama. That's what Royce always said about them, and he was the oldest. Their crew knew one another since high school. Their bond was super strong, and even when they parted ways for a few years it didn't make their bond less strong. They did crazy shit. Hell, Brew served time for a few months on an assault charge. One he would do over and over again. He shook his head and looked toward the doorway. Why the fuck was he thinking about his past and how fucked up his life could have been if it weren't for his friends?

The moment she came into view he felt his throat tighten up and then Train whistled. "No wonder Logic was feeling horny. The woman looks like a fucking model," Train said.

Brew took in the sight of Alda. Long black dress that hugged her figure so tight they could tell she had super hard abs and one round, sexy ass that was more than a handful. The V of the dress slid tight against those breasts and up over her shoulders, revealing more skin, and as she turned, smiling, her thick brown hair bounced around her shoulders and he saw the high slit up the side of her dress. Nothing but tan thigh and a sexy pair of black high heels. Before they were even halfway into the club the guys were drooling and offering her drinks. She ignored them, as Donata and Alessa, who were just as attractive and sexy, headed straight toward the bar and Dominick, Giada and Royce. He watched Royce's eyes take in the sight of Alda and that jealous feeling Brew had as the men offered her drinks didn't hit him when Royce looked at Alda, instead it aroused him. They were all denying these feelings, this attraction to sweet, sexy Alda. Licking his lips, he looked at Train.

"We're out of our fucking minds. You know that, right? We can't. We just fucking can't," Train said.

He heard how conflicted Train sounded. The whole do the right thing and respect their bosses' girlfriend's friend was starting to feel like some stupid excuse. If the woman wanted to fuck around with them and explore this attraction they all felt, why stop it? They were adults. Hell, he and the others had a good ten years plus on Alda. Maybe that was the thing that bothered them. Would they taint her youth, her inexperience and sweetness? Make her into some slut, or bad girl who did four guys? They couldn't offer her a commitment like their bosses had with Giada. They just weren't those types of men. They were fighters, warriors, fucking killers. They did bad shit. They beat people up, threatened people, put pressure on them when needed. They had reputations. A woman, other than one to seek satisfaction of their needs, was not going to fit into their lives.

He stared at her, and after Giada and Dominick greeted her and Donata and Alessa did, too, Royce changed positions, kissed her cheek hello and ran his palm along her hip and over her ass.

"Let's go say hello," Train said and Brew shot a look at him as Train rubbed his hands together then headed that way.

* * * *

Royce slid his palm along Alda's waist and stared down into her eyes, but the low dip in her dress and her abundant breasts forced his eyes to linger there as he bent lower to kiss her cheek. She smelled incredible and looked like some sort of supermodel. Her hair bounced, hitting his neck and as he eased back she looked intimidated. Boy, did that do a number to his cock.

"Good to see you, Alda," he said and she gave a soft smile then turned away from him. It was kind of rude, and he wondered why she did that. She wasn't snobby or stuck-up, she was likable and nice, which he wasn't at all. Complete opposites.

Before he could process her reaction to him Train approached, along with Brew. They greeted the women and Royce took the opportunity to watch Alda as Train kissed her cheek hello and then Brew did the same thing. Both men remained next to her as Dominick ordered a round of drinks.

"I'm good, Dom, I should head back over to keep eyes on things," Royce said to him.

"Enjoy yourself a little, Royce. The bouncers are there for a reason and they got it covered," Dominick said to him.

He looked at Alda, who took the drink Dominick ordered for her and the ladies and handed them out from the bartender and then he noticed the men checking out Alda's ass as she stood there. Two guys slid by her, slightly bumping her. She turned and the guys smiled. "Hey," one said and she looked away. Royce saw the disappointment in their eyes. The woman was a magnet for horny men, yet she blew them off with ease and experience as if bored. Royce wondered if she was easy but just played hard to get. Then his gut clenched and he thought the idea felt all wrong.

Royce was not happy about the way he was feeling. He was a man who liked to keep to himself. He did his job protecting the bosses and doing whatever was necessary to help them and the surrounding connected families. He didn't like conflict but handled it head on. He didn't date and hadn't been with a woman in a few weeks. The last time he was with one she knew better than to bother him again. That woman sure wasn't Alda.

He noticed Train kept a hand at her lower back and even caressed her, whispered things to her and she smirked and then squinted at him like he was teasing her. It appeared playful but his thoughts were purely lustful. When Alda didn't move but instead kept talking and adding comments to the conversation it made Royce think about touching her, too. Immediately he felt like a scumbag. She wasn't the type of woman he and the guys sought relief with. Plus, she seemed scared of them, even uninterested like maybe they weren't good enough because of their line of work. She didn't know that they were wealthy men. Had been business partners with their bosses and others, and were actually more than just head security. They chose to be by the Coglonie men's sides because the Coglonies trusted them to protect them and Giada a hundred percent.

Maybe she was stuck-up after all?

* * * *

Alda was shaking. What was with the sudden pushy flirtatiousness among the four men she avoided like a disease? Starting with Logic at Oliva, and now here with Royce, Train, and Brew. Well, not Royce. That man had a killer look in his eyes and on his face at all times. In fact right now he was in a dead stare at her, looking suspicious of her. She gulped and looked away a moment until Train asked her if pomegranate martinis were her favorite. Train was as big as a brick house and Brew, hell, he was stocky, muscular and supposedly covered in crazy tattoos. It didn't help that she knew a woman who had a wild night with Brew. That his tattoos were fierce looking. It made her feel uncomfortable and like these men were after sex and nothing more. The woman told her that Brew was wild in bed, demanded control and when they were done he reminded her to never contact him again or even try to approach him. He said if he was interested in doing anything else with her again, that he would let her know.

Alda slid away from Train and Brew and then pretended that she needed to tell Giada something. It seemed to work as a few minutes passed and they walked away.

"Scared them off. Was that on purpose?" Giada whispered to her.

"What do you mean?" she asked.

"Don't 'what do you mean' me. They are interested in you and I'm shocked."

"Oh really, why is that?"

"Because they do not date. They don't ever show any sort of interest in any woman in front of anyone, and they don't talk much. Except to me. I make them talk and it drives them crazy. Dominick warned me to not piss them off and so I don't push so much anymore," Giada said and smiled as she winked.

"We were over at Oliva's bar and I saw Logic. He was…attentive," she told Giada. Giada's eyes widened.

"Attentive, huh? Hmm, I wonder if they decided their attraction to you is too hard to ignore. Maybe this sexy model body has them all wild with desire," she said to her and eyed over her dress.

"I don't think so. I keep meeting one jerk after the next. It's boring and you know what, work is crazy right now, too. I shouldn't even be out tonight. I was just hoping it would make me tired enough to sleep through the night."

Giada squinted at her. "What's going on?"

Alda exhaled. "Just a new product we're getting ready to launch, the designers haven't come up with anything the bosses want or like, and the bosses are talking international sales. It's insane."

Now Dominick joined the conversation and looked at Alda then behind her. Brew, Train, and Royce stepped closer and surrounded her, Giada and Dominick.

"International sales? That could be great. Would you be involved with that and travel abroad?" Giada asked.

"I don't know. That hasn't exactly been my luck in the previous companies I've worked for," she said and took a sip from her drink.

"What do you mean?" Dominick asked her.

"I've worked for a few companies, small ones like MAX Industries, and when we had a product take off some bigger company would come in and buy us out," she told them.

"That's typical. Do you at least get some sort of severance package?" Train asked her.

"Yes, I have in the past and thank goodness it's been enough to hold me over financially until the next job. I'm just getting tired of it. I like the smaller businesses and helping to create and promote the products, but then it's kind of disappointing not seeing it through to the life of the product. I don't know, maybe I'm just losing that cut throat attitude necessary with this type of work," she said and then took a sip of her martini.

"It can be frustrating, I'm sure. Ever think about starting your own company? Any products or ideas you have that you want to promote or introduce to the world?" Giada asked her.

She gave Giada a sideways glance and exhaled.

"What? Did we miss something?" Royce asked very seriously as if offended or like he was left out of an inside joke.

"Oh, Alda has a few dreams of what she would really like to do. She's talked about them for years but—"

"But, I am in no financial position to take that kind of chance and risk. It's silly stuff. Besides, I'm working for the company right now and who knows what interesting things might happen in the next month or so," she said to them.

"Yeah, you could be a world traveler, having to fly overseas to promote the products. It's a makeup line, right? Maybe Milan, Italy?" Giada asked, all smiles. Alda smiled and then chuckled.

"I could see Alda rubbing shoulders with models and the fashion gurus," Donata said, joining the conversation.

Then Dominick's cell phone went off, he pulled it out to answer it and then stood up.

"I need to take care of something. Royce, come with me, Brew, remain here with Giada for fifteen minutes longer and then bring her upstairs," Dominick ordered.

Alda swallowed hard as Dominick gave Giada a kiss and then told her to listen to Brew and come upstairs when he said to. Dominick held her chin and then stroked her jaw and kissed her softly, his expression firm. Giada nodded, and then the men disappeared.

Brew's expression never changed throughout the entire thing. He merely looked concerned and then took the orders from Dominick. Giada would have to leave them in fifteen minutes. Alda exhaled.

"I hope everything is okay," Alda said to Giada.

"It's not your concern. Enjoy the extra time with Giada before I bring her upstairs," Brew said to her, his attitude completely different than just a few minutes ago. Giada gave Alda a smile.

"So, can we do dinner Friday night or are you too crazy with things at work? I'd like for you to visit with Gisella and I at Club Empire," Giada said to her.

"I think Donata and Alessa were debating about going there too but for drinks. They're both working late but wanted to meet up."

"Well, plan on meeting me there for dinner. Gisella needs a little help with something at the club. A promotional event," Giada told her and winked.

"Seriously?" Alda asked and then Brew reached for his phone, glanced at it and then looked at Giada.

"It's time to head up."

"Already? Can't I stay a little longer?" she asked and Brew raised one of his eyebrows at her. She nodded then took Alda's hands.

"I'll call you to confirm a time Friday night. Hope you can make it there."

"I will. Hope all is well."

"No worries, Alda," Giada said and then said good-bye to Alessa and Donata.

Alda watched them go and she felt the odd sensations fill her belly. She couldn't imagine being involved with a made man, never mind multiple men like Giada was. To have to listen to their orders, and stop enjoying fun with close friends because a boyfriend had something going on and didn't want her out of his sight. That thought gave her a surprisingly different reaction. She wondered what it would feel like to have a man or multiple men care for her so much they didn't want her out of their sights. Would it be annoying, or would it be arousing? Could she stand to give up control and allow men to direct her every move? No freaking way. Then again, Giada wasn't doing that. She gave Dominick, Giuseppe, and Andreas a run for their money and didn't always comply with their rules, but it got her into trouble. They could have lost her, so maybe that was why when any of them gave an order or expected her to remain nearby she complied. After all, it was quite obvious that the men loved Giada and she loved them. Alda respected that and for some reason she felt envious.

Then she thought about Brew and the others. When they were beckoned they had to leave immediately. It didn't matter what was going on or whom they were with. A woman wouldn't mean anything to them but instant pleasure, nothing more. She could get a man like that anywhere. She needed to ignore this attraction and just focus on what she needed and wanted. Obviously Logic was after a good time, and she fell for it. Brew had a reputation and was probably the same. After a piece of ass. Train, well, he was huge, quiet and demanding.

Royce was downright intimidating most of all. Who was she kidding? They were all intimidating. So why couldn't she stop her body's reaction to them every time they were around? It would be smarter to ignore then. Definitely.

"One more round, Alda, then we're hitting the dance floor," Donata said to her and Alessa cheered and they clinked glasses. She smiled and cheered, too. She was young and single. What was better than that?

Chapter 2

Salento Sorenno gave Lou Carvetti the stare down. "You think this is going to work for much longer? It was supposed to be a very private clientele," Salento stated.

"Hey, who would have thought there would be such a demand for this drug? Most men are afraid of getting busted for using it on a woman to get her into bed," Lou said to him.

"This form is strong shit. It wipes out the memory and basically as long as the guy is careful the woman is none the wiser. What I don't like is how many more calls of inquiry I'm getting. You know he's in town. Got in last night."

Lou Carvetti widened his eyes. "He's in New York? What the hell? Why? Doesn't he trust us?" Carvetti asked.

"Seems like maybe he doesn't and wants to make sure no one is skimming off the top or taking samples," Salento stated.

"It's all good. I don't need drugs to get a woman into bed," Lou Carvetti said, leaned back in the chair and licked his lower lip, staring at Salento.

"No one said you did. I for one think it's a fucking game. The boss may want to put a hold on any more distribution for a little spell of time."

"What? Why the hell would he want to do that?" Carvetti asked.

"Pump up the price. Supply and demand, or weed out anyone who may be trying to push a similar product."

"Smart. So I gather you want me and the guys to keep an ear out for similar product just in case?"

"Yes. Anything pops up, eliminate it quickly. Understood?"

"Yes. Got it," Lou Carvetti said and hoped no one was stupid enough to mess with them. If they chose to try and pry their way into their boss's, Titanium, as he liked to be called, business, then they were as good as dead. Carvetti and his men would be the ones to eliminate them.

* * * *

"This is not going to go over well at all, Lisa. It's trash. What have Benny and you been up to for the last several weeks?" Alda Ruffinno asked her co-worker. Alda was looking at design labels for the new line of cosmetic products coming out in a couple of months for MAX, a company that now had over fifty different products, from makeup and perfumes to designer bags. Alda held the position of assistant sales, creative marketing and design manager. Really a job for more than one person but the company was small and her bosses were cheap.

"Oh no, are you serious? What's wrong with it? I mean, I know the printing is slightly off and all but it adds a sort of hip aspect to the design," Lisa countered and Alda knew it was because Lisa worked on this with Benny for several weeks, and the two of them were an item.

"Hip? Seriously? That's not what came to mind when I looked at it and you know as well as I do that Haley is going to hate it, never mind Maxwell, he'll cringe."

"What should we do then? I'm all out of ideas. Everything we've presented to them has been turned down."

"No, Lisa, not completely turned down. Haley and Maxwell liked this aspect and they liked the colors. That was the hardest part, going through the color palette and coming up with one area to focus on. Might I suggest you straighten out the wording, add more color alternating light purple and violet with a hint of bluish purple. Make that flower stand out bold as well as the brand name MAX," she said.

"I don't know what you mean," Lisa stated and Alda bent over to show her on paper and to compare the designs. She brought up color palettes and then started to rearrange the designs right there on the computer.

"See how this stands out more? Each petal is bold, fresh, real, just like the makeup behind the label. That's what Maxwell and Haley are looking for."

"Now this is a pleasurable sight indeed."

They heard the voice and Alda looked over her shoulder to see Maxwell standing there smirking with his hands on his hips, but it was the other man next to him that caught Alda's eye. Apparently Lisa's, too, as she quickly introduced herself.

Alda, on the other hand, glanced back at the screen. A few more tweaks and changes. She pressed a couple of buttons and dragged along the mouse then saved the design.

"Alda, I would like you to meet Antonio Sparks." When Max said the man's name Alda gasped and then turned to look at him.

Antonio Sparks was a very wealthy businessman, among other things. He was also involved with international sales. Maxwell and Haley were trying to get their products noticed overseas. Antonio was a gambling sort of man. One that bought out companies or helped build them up, taking more than fifty percent of the profit. She wondered what Maxwell and Haley were doing discussing business with him. Hopefully not selling off the company. *Here we go again.*

She stepped away from the computer but then Antonio and Maxwell came closer. She reached out her hand and locked gazes with the very handsome older man. His hair was jet black with a dusting of light gray along the sides. It gave him character and made him look distinguished. Their hands touched and she felt an attraction to him. He must have as well as he squinted and then gazed over her body. She was dressed for the evening out with friends. All she had to do was remove the slim fitting sweater that covered her low dip in front of her black dress, and she was ready for the visit to Club

Empire and dinner with Giada and Gisella. Antonio stared at her and held her hand a bit too longer than necessary. As she pulled back she noticed the tattoo on his hand, but couldn't tell what it was from just a glimpse. He dressed designer, and looked to have a nice set of muscles under the suit he wore. She turned away and slid her hand along her waist.

"Nice to meet you, sir," she said and then Maxwell slammed his hand down on the table.

"This is it! This. Is. It," he exclaimed and then looked at her and smiled.

"You did this, right? You came up with this idea? I heard you as we came in. My God, Alda, you are amazing and I love it. Haley will love it, too. Let me call her down here."

Maxwell was so excited and when Alda looked at Lisa, Lisa lipped the words *thank you*. Alda nodded.

Maxwell looked at Antonio, who was staring into Alda's eyes.

"What do you think, Antonio? Brilliant? Eye catching? Unique? What?" he asked but Antonio stared at her.

"All of the above and then some," he said, never taking his eyes off of her and totally flirting.

Maxwell chuckled.

"Indeed, Alda is an exceptional woman, and she will be joining us for dinner and dancing at Club Empire tonight to celebrate the label being finalized and of course discussing the opportunities overseas," Maxwell told Antonio as Haley entered the office.

"What's going on, Maxwell?" Haley asked, looking and sounding annoyed.

Alda was trying to process Maxwell's words and something about attending dinner tonight and business overseas.

"Look," he said and pointed to the screen.

The older woman with her gray blonde hair had an aura of arrogance and snobbiness about her. Alda got along with her okay but the woman definitely was at the top of the bitch-o-meter. She eyed Alda over, winked up at Antonio and then approached the computer.

She was silent a moment and Lisa's face went white and she gulped. Alda remained somewhat relaxed. If Haley didn't like this design then Alda was at a loss.

"Ohhh. This is perfect," Haley whispered and tilted her head and then looked at Alda. "You are so talented, Alda. I swear, is there anything you can't do?" she asked, but her tone seemed jealous. Alda didn't know what was up with that.

She glanced at Maxwell and Antonio. "She looks very capable. Are you head of designs here at MAX?" Antonio asked.

"Not head of designs but assistant manager of sales and creative marketing. Indeed, she is very capable of all the roles she plays with this company, and Alda created this besides a wonderful game plan on advertising for the release of my new cosmetics line, just like her unique sales strategies for the other products. She completely understood my desires," Maxwell said, not even hearing or seeing what was going on here. Not Antonio's blatant flirtatious comments or Haley's jealous attitude. Sometimes Alda wondered why she even worked here. She wished there were other opportunities but there weren't right now. She would love getting involved with creative designs for major products and even helping with advertising commercials, print ads, etc. She was very creative indeed.

"Things may work out, Haley. I'm in," Antonio said to Haley but his eyes roamed over Alda's body.

Then Haley completely confused her as Haley looked at Antonio and nodded. Haley gave Alda's arm a squeeze. It was crazy.

"Exceptional work, Alda. We leave at six for Club Empire. Why don't you plan on coming along in the limo with the three of us? We can discuss some plans Maxwell and I have been discussing with Antonio. I'll have Bernice change the reservations for four instead of three of us. See you in the lobby within the hour," Haley said and then took Antonio's arm and led him out of the office as she carried on about Club Empire.

Maxwell grabbed Alda's hand.

"I'm so impressed and Haley is, too, that's for sure. She will expect you to cooperate tonight. Antonio Sparks is a very wealthy and powerful man. He can help to advance your career, as well. However, after seeing what you came up with for my cosmetics line, I'm going to fight that man tooth and nail," Maxwell said and winked before he headed out of the office.

Alda was a little confused. What did he mean by Antonio advancing her career, and about Maxwell fighting him tooth and nail for her?

"Oh God, that man is super sexy hot. He was totally checking you out, Alda," Lisa said to her.

Alda licked her lower lip, her eyes still squinting in confusion about what exactly just took place here. "Are you okay?" Lisa asked her.

"Uhm, I don't know. What did you get out of their remarks?" she asked Lisa then saved the design on the computer under its own file and then forwarded it to Lisa's e-mail.

Lisa looked toward the empty doorway, and then looked to be sure no one was there. She turned around to face Alda.

"Well, for one, Antonio Sparks is totally interested in you. Two, Maxwell loved your design and so did Haley, which is a miracle in itself, and three, something was definitely exchanged between Haley and Antonio and it seemed over you. The man gave a nod, she complied and now you're going to dinner at that new club," Lisa said.

Alda felt uneasy. She didn't like conflicts, or problems. She liked things to run smoothly and when faced with a challenge she took a roundabout way to solve it unless push came to shove and then she attacked. The last year had been an emotional one with a few of her close friends getting involved in ménage relationships and facing dangers. She wasn't like them. She couldn't handle danger, confrontation, trouble in any form. She liked her simple life, her small apartment located in the same building as an elementary school, her circle of friends and the comfort being around them gave her as her only family, and this job.

She'd worked here for over a year now, having moved from one company to another after they were bought out by larger companies. Her resume showed her professionalism and experience but despite the successes whenever she interviewed she had to explain about the companies being bought out, not failing. She wished one of the larger companies had held on to her and offered her something great. Instead she got exceptional severance packages which took off the stresses of finding work immediately. She could pick and choose. She chose MAX Industries because it was a new, up and coming company and product that needed branding, promotions and the products were great. She used a lot of them herself. There was potential for expansion and with owners like Haley and Maxwell there was no way either owner was going to let some larger company force them into selling to be bought out. No way, these two wanted fortune, fame and exposure.

"It will be fine, Alda. You can handle this. You've worked here over a year and in that time have truly helped to push the products and get them into the public eye. You even got famous people to promote the products. You'll be fine. Haley and Max adore you," Lisa said and stood by her desk.

"Adore me is taking it too far. They like what I have done for the company, but we all know the second any of us screws up, we're outta here," Alda said to her.

"Yes, which reminds me that you saved our asses. Benny and mine. We owe you big time," Lisa said then walked out of the office.

Alda glanced at her watch. Forty minutes until she needed to be downstairs and then do dinner with the bosses and this Antonio guy. At Club Empire, no less. She needed to text Giada and let her know she couldn't do dinner but hopefully drinks and why. She was supposed to meet Donata and Alessa at Club X around eight. She would tell them to meet her at Club Empire instead.

She pulled out her cell phone and texted all of them. They responded quickly. She swallowed hard when she thought about this business dinner. The whole way this all went down made her nervous, suspicious, but she didn't have much of a choice. She needed to go. Hopefully it all worked out accordingly.

* * * *

Antonio Sparks couldn't take his eyes off of Alda Raffinno. She was stunning, sexy, classy, and her body absolute perfection. Those green eyes were dark, mesmerizing and drew him in as she spoke. She really knew her stuff, but he didn't care. She was exactly what he had been searching for. He could hardly contain the excitement he felt. Years. It took years to finally find her, and he was shocked that it was in a business setting, and unprovoked, completely natural, like fate.

He nodded as she explained her ideas about advertising overseas and about warehouse locations and things that were beyond her position here. Haley, who he'd known for many years, was using this woman. There was no doubt in Antonio's mind. "Haley, I sure do hope that you're paying Alda an obscene amount of money, because I can tell you right now, if she worked for me she would be a partner," he said, and by the blush to Alda's cheeks, he shocked her and maybe even won some points.

"Funny you bring that up, Antonio, not that it's any of your business, or that we would allow you to take her from us, but she is due for a very large bonus. Max and I were going to surprise her with it on Monday, but seeing you brought this up," Haley said and looked at Max, who smiled wide and placed his hand over Alda's hand and squeezed it. Antonio's chest tightened and he clenched his teeth. No one should be touching her. She was going to be his. He found her. Holy shit, after all the others, he found her.

"Alda, we have been so impressed with your professionalism, your work ethic and all you've done to bring MAX Industries to the public eye, and sales to an all-time high. Things are only going to get better, and Haley and I would like to offer you a new role, an increase in pay and a bonus for all you've accomplished."

"A new role, and bonus? So you're not planning on selling the company?" she asked.

"Selling the company? No way. We've worked so hard to establish this company," Max said, looking shocked and then glanced at Antonio, who had a small grin. He could easily take this company from Haley and she knew it. Max was a dreamer, not a businessman.

"Antonio is here to discuss our possible future deal with him and opening additional warehouses and offices overseas to the UK. An expansion of sorts. Which brings me back to you," he said and winked. Antonio narrowed his eyes at Max. He hoped the man wasn't some sort of competition. She was gorgeous and when they arrived at this Club Empire, a very upscale venue, he noticed the men immediately looking at her and a few others in particular knew her and greeted them. Including Collin Fiorre, some sort of modern day organized crime boss. His sweet beauty seemed to have friends in low places, but so did he.

"Seeing the stunned expression on your face, I take it you haven't looked at your direct deposit amount that went out today. You'll see an additional twenty thousand dollar bonus, as well as a new salary of three hundred thousand," Max said and smiled. Antonio watched her expression and then the hand cover her mouth, her eyes widen and tears fill her eyes. Max released her hand and smiled wide.

"I told you she would be shocked, Haley. Alda, it's been long coming, and well deserved. Let's make a toast," he said. She uncovered her mouth and then shook her head.

"I don't know what to say. I can't believe this. I was so worried that tonight would be about losing my job and a takeover. My God, I'm shaking," she said and lifted her hand and it was quite obvious she was shaking. Antonio reached out and took her hand. She looked at him, surprised.

"It's going to be a pleasure working with you, Alda. Your honesty, straightforwardness and all around beauty will be a pleasure, I'm certain," he said and then placed her hand on his thigh and then waved with his hand for the waiter to bring over the champagne. He popped the cork and they all laughed and cheered as the waiter poured the glasses. He released her hand and then lifted the glass. Max made the toast.

"To MAX Industries and all that is yet to come," Max said and they clinked their glasses together and took sips of champagne. Antonio slid his arm over the back of her chair and looked at Haley and winked.

Haley squinted but smiled softly. She knew what was coming. MAX Industries was more than just a company selling perfumes, makeup, and accessories, it was their little front for so much more. Haley would be getting one of his own special thank you's later this evening in bed.

* * * *

"Who's the big shot dick with the designer suit?" Logic asked Lenox, one of Collin and Fedarro's security guys.

"Businesspeople Alda works with. I think the woman and the big guy are her bosses, and the other one I don't know. They're celebrating though, as you just saw. Alda looks emotional," Lenox said and took a sip from his drink.

"She was supposed to meet Gisella and Giada here for dinner then had to change plans. I wonder if she'll stay with those people all night instead," Logic asked and watched them.

Lenox gave his arm a nudge.

"Alda is gorgeous," Lenox said to him and Logic looked at him and mumbled.

"Don't tell me you don't think she's hot," Lenox asked him.

"If who is hot?" Ziek asked, joining them. Lenox looked at him and Logic exhaled. He couldn't believe how jealous he felt watching Alda talking with the other man and the guy's arm was around her chair and he kept whispering to her. She was smiling and they were all drinking champagne. He should realize she wasn't right for him and the guys. She could be traveling overseas if her conversation with Giada was correct that Brew informed him about. Plus she wanted to maybe start her own business. She was the commitment kind of woman. They didn't do commitments. Couldn't do them. Brew said she had an odd reaction when Dominick ordered the other guys to leave the bar and follow him. Then gave Giada orders and a time limit of fifteen minutes. Brew said Alda looked shocked. She definitely wouldn't be able to handle being involved with enforcers.

"We're talking about Alda. She looks incredible as usual. When she walked in wearing that navy blue dress and her breasts pouring from the top, they're so fucking big, never mind her ass," Lenox said.

"Oh yeah, who didn't see it? The woman turns heads," Ziek said.

"Hey." Logic raised his voice and narrowed his eyes at them. Both men didn't even flinch. Ziek smirked.

"Told you," Lenox said.

"Damn. You make a move yet, Logic?" Ziek asked.

"No! What the fuck, man?" he asked and scrunched his face up then took a slug of beer.

"Why the hell not? She's fire," Lenox asked.

"You two know why the fuck not," Logic said to them.

"Not really. She's super hot and sexy. Any man would love to tap that. I don't get you," Ziek said to him.

"Sure you don't. It's the same reason why you two, Cobra and Roman haven't moved in on Alessa," Logic said to them and saw them both scrunch their eyes as if pissed and then exhale. They took drinks from their beer bottles.

"There ya go. Enforcers don't fucking date," Logic added.

The sound of laughter drew their attention to the left and there was Alessa surrounded by four men who worked for Tudoro Garlitto.

"Fucking dicks. They were hitting on her last week, too," Lenox said to them.

"Why don't you go over there and take her away from them," Logic teased.

"Same fucking reason you won't go over to that table, throw Alda over your shoulder and take her out of here and to your place," Ziek said and they all mumbled.

This was definitely a sucky situation for all of them. Logic wondered if there was some way it could work out, or maybe if he could just get a little taste of Alda, he might be able to get her out of his head? Maybe?

* * * *

Alda was ecstatic, and once Antonio, Haley and Max left the club she was able to join her friends. Or so she thought. As she made her way across the dance floor and toward the bar where Donata, Gisella, and the men were, she spotted Alessa talking to two guys who worked for Tudoro Garlitto, Micky and Spence as well as her cousins C.J. and Randy. Right beside them were Brendan and Fogerty and she immediately caught their attention. She couldn't not go over as Alessa gave her a wave and widened her eyes in one of those "help me" expressions she gave when she didn't want to be rude but really wasn't interested in the men hitting on her. Thank goodness, because her cousins would be in a heap of trouble. Lenox and Ziek were in a dead stare at Alessa right now and only a few feet away at the bar closest to where they stood.

"Damn, woman, you get sexier each time I see you," Fogerty said to her but she bypassed him and went to C.J., who gave Fogerty a dirty look then pulled her into his arms. He kissed her cheek and then let her go to Randy next. Her cousins looked good, but she didn't like them hanging with these men.

The arm wrapped around her waist quickly and Fogerty kissed her shoulder and whispered into her ear. She could smell the alcohol on his breath.

"You just made my night a hell of a lot better. Dance with me, baby," he said to her.

She pushed down on his hands. "I don't think so, Fogerty," she said and stepped away from him only for Brendan to take her hand and pull her into an embrace.

"How are you, Alda?" he asked, and held her against him a few seconds too long. He stared down into her eyes and licked his lower lip. He had hit on her several times before and she blew him off. He was a player, and a drug dealer. Her cousins shouldn't be hanging out with these men. She hoped they weren't working with him and for Mickey and Spence.

She pushed away from him and gave a medium smile. "Good. What's going on with you guys? What are you doing here?" she asked, stepping back in an attempt to put distance between her and them. Why men thought they could touch any woman they wanted and act possessive, she didn't understand. It annoyed her, except when she liked the guy, of course. Instantly, Train, Royce, Brew and Logic popped into her head. Caught off guard at her thought process, she felt the hand take her hand and it was Mickey. He stared down at her.

"No kiss hello for me?" he asked.

"Seriously? I just saw you the other night," she said and sort of rolled her eyes at him, looking away, turning, but his hold tightened and he pulled her closer and off balance. She placed her palm against his chest so she wouldn't fall.

"I look forward to your kisses," he said.

"Cool it, Mickey," her cousin C.J. chimed in, finally, and Mickey gave her cousins a dirty look as if reminding them of who was more powerful. Maybe in the Garlitto family, but her cousins weren't connected at all. They had no power, which made her wonder why she kept seeing them with these two men and Brendan and Fogerty. She didn't like them.

"We're discussing some business things, Alda, so maybe you should be a bit more polite for your cousins' sakes," Fogerty threatened in a tone that made her gut clench. *What possible business would you and my cousins have with these men?* She wanted to ask, but kept her mouth shut. C.J. and Randy were older than her, men, and they chose this path of life, not her.

She gave him a dirty look.

"In that case, Alessa, want to go talk with Giada and Gisella?" she asked.

Spence pulled Alessa close.

"We were making some progress, Alda. Stay here, too," Mickey said to Alda. She looked at Alessa, who definitely looked a bit timid. Not that Alda wasn't. The men were connected to the Garlitto family. She needed to keep things calm. One look behind Alessa and the group and toward the bar and Alda saw Lenox and Ziek staring toward them. That had potential for trouble.

"We have to go. We were supposed to hang with the girls earlier but I had a business dinner," she said to them and took Alessa's hand. "Come on so we can catch up with the girls."

As she started to walk away with Alessa she felt the arm go around her waist and haul her back. C.J. stepped forward. "Fogerty, let her go," he said and Fogerty whispered into her ear.

"Playing hard to get now. I've seen you on the dance floor, baby. I heard you don't date. Maybe you just like to fuck. We'd be good together," he said and she pulled from his arms, he laughed and kept a hold on her and she slapped his face. He went to grab her and a hand grabbed his arms and abruptly turned him around. The dark, intense expression on Royce Brooks's face shocked her, but it was how quickly he struck Fogerty, and knocked Fogerty on his ass that made her jaw drop and her heart race. C.J. grabbed Alda and then Train grabbed C.J., telling him to get off of her.

She placed her palm against Train's chest and pressed close to him as C.J. still held her arm lightly but took a semi-retreating step back.

"No, Train, this is my cousin," she said to him and Train's dark eyes widened and then he glared at C.J.

"You're her cousin and you let this dick fucking touch her?" he reprimanded.

Royce went to grab C.J. and she put herself between Royce and C.J.

"No, Royce, it's okay. He's my cousin," she said to him, felt his hard muscles beneath her hand as she pressed her palm against his chest and her palm ached. She pulled back and hissed then held it to her chest.

"What's going on?" Logic, Brew, Lenox and Ziek joined them.

"It's over. Let's move now. You assholes leave these two ladies alone," Royce ordered and Fogerty gave him a dirty look then smirked as he looked at Alda.

"Didn't know she was your bitch, Royce. Now we do," he said and then turned away and walked to the bar with Mickey, Spence and Brendan.

The expression on Royce's face made her shake. Tears filled her eyes and her gut clenched as if the glimpse into Royce's temper and abilities shocked her speechless. The man was capable, quick, resourceful like some soldier. He stepped into action to help her and embarrassment struck and concern of what he may think. Especially as Fogerty called her Royce's bitch.

Royce rubbed her arm and she jerked, pulling back only for him to slide his other arm to her hip and squeeze, keeping her in place. Those dark brown eyes, gruff along his chin and cheeks, the vein pulsating by his temple and the feel of his extra large, hard hand on her body, added to his ominous persona.

"You okay?" he asked. She nodded, and stared up at the monstrosity of a man who was filled with muscles. She could see his neck muscles in the tight shirt he wore. His dark brown eyes, wide shoulders and crew cut hair made him look military. She didn't think he ever served, but what did she know.

Lenox and Ziek walked Alessa away and Alda looked at her cousins as Logic, Train, Royce, and Brew all gathered around them.

"Sorry, Alda. Fogerty drank too much and was being an asshole. Will you be okay with these guys?" C.J. asked her.

"She's obviously safer with us," Brew barked at him.

"Of course I'm fine. Maybe you and Randy shouldn't be hanging out with him. Maybe he'll only get you into trouble," she said to C.J. He looked her over, then looked at the guys surrounding her like she was important and they were her personal security team. She gulped.

"We'll talk tomorrow," C.J. said to her.

"C.J., Randy, leave here. Whatever is going on with you and those men—"

Royce gripped her shoulders and she leaned back as if needing his strength to deal with her cousins. C.J. narrowed his eyes at her.

"This isn't the time to talk. I'll call you tomorrow," he said and then gave the men dirty looks and he and Randy walked away.

Royce turned her away from them and looked down into her eyes.

"Cousins, huh?" he questioned, as if not believing her.

"Stupid ones, apparently," she said and started to pull away from him to put some distance between them.

Brew reached for her hand.

"You okay, slugger?" he asked and she shook her head, and willed the tears away. She wasn't going to let those men ruin her night. She wanted to celebrate with her friends. She was getting a raise, a promotion and the company wasn't being sold off. If her cousins wanted to hang out with thugs and pretend to be made men, what was she to do? She felt guilty suddenly and knew this wouldn't end here tonight. She would talk to them this week. Hound them until they promised to stay away from Fogerty and Brendan.

Royce reached over and cupped her cheek.

"Those guys are assholes. Don't ever talk to them again. Understand me?" he ordered.

"Two of them are my cousins," she said and Train slid his hand to her hip and squeezed.

"They didn't protect you from those guys. Unacceptable," he said.

"Come on, let's go over toward the others," Logic suggested and they all walked to the bar and Giada and Gisella asked what happened and Alessa explained. All the while Train kept a hold on her hip and Brew, Logic, and Train stared at her, making her feel like they were trying to read her mind. She had to be smart here. They weren't the commitment types and no matter how much she liked them and was attracted to them, she needed to see this for what it was. Nothing. Hanging out with them and letting them touch her, hold her, protect her would make other people think she really was their woman, or how Fogerty said, their bitch. No way. She wanted more. Had more respect for her body, for her reputation and for everything she worked for. Lust wasn't going to make her do something stupid.

Chapter 3

Royce was half paying attention to the conversation between Brew and Andreas over some ultimate fighting event that was going to be on next Saturday. They disagreed over who would take the title and win the big match. The other guys threw in their comments, but Royce's mind drifted to last week. He was getting pissed at himself thinking about Alda so much. She wasn't capable of taking care of herself. Men watched her, wanted her, and those dicks would have forced her to remain with them all night if he hadn't stepped in with Train and the others. That pissed him off. So did how quickly Alda became quiet, closed up and then headed out early.

He tried to focus on the new responsibilities he and the team would have. Dominick, Giuseppe, and Andreas were assigning family members to Giada's security and Royce and his team had been training them the last month so that they could keep watch at the other clubs like Oliva, to make sure they stayed top notch. Their bosses and the other bosses in the Fiorre family didn't want the drugs, the prostitutes and other shit in the clubs or at least not so noticeable.

They didn't want to risk any cops coming snooping around. They had their inside people in the departments and would catch wind, hopefully, of any operations, and they kept the clubs as clean as they could. Other clubs had reputations of being the spots to be for that kind of shit. Their clubs and bars were upscale and tended to draw in the wealthier clientele, as well as more professional men and women. That thought brought Royce's mind back to Alda.

Holy shit, he never thought about any woman as much as he thought about her. Royce was starting to think that if he just made a move and screwed her already maybe he could get her out of his head. But every time he thought that thought out of frustration for this foreign reaction to this woman, he felt guilty and lower than dog shit. She was not some whore. She was a professional, young...fuck, very young woman with the body of a model, well, pin-up model, not super thin and no brains. Every conversation with her, or that he listened to as she spoke, she came across so worldly, professional and sweet. Maybe that was it. Maybe he was getting tired of the bad girls, the wild ones who let him achieve the release he needed and especially after having to do crazy shit in this line of work. Every time he got his adrenaline pumping, had to knock someone around or put them in their place, that need to claim, to conquer would become overwhelming. Sometimes if it was accessible, sex would lessen that deep inner need, yet lately it was getting worse and he knew why. Alda. Just the thought of her did something to his insides. Royce was pissed off about it. A woman? A five foot six, sexual goddess was doing this to him? Fuck.

Brew was bullshitting with Andreas, Cobra, Rogan and Maverick until the bosses spoke to them about their responsibilities and some new security measures at the clubs.

Morano, Collin, Dominick, Major and Sunny were discussing business deals and some rumors about drugs making their way into their businesses and ways to stop them, especially as it seemed someone not connected to the family was supplying.

"Well, first of all, what exactly are they selling? That would help us narrow down who these assholes are," Brew asked the bosses.

"That's the problem, Brew, it's something new. This is just buzz we've gotten wind of from other club owners. I don't want this shit at any of our places," Collin stated very seriously.

"Of course not, but if we don't know what to look for, how can we stop it from coming into our places?" Brew asked.

"That's why we need to put out some feelers, and keep your eyes open. Get security on top of the customers more. Use the surveillance videos, improve that at each place so if something goes down, or we hear about what this shit is, we may catch them on surveillance video," Morano stated.

"This is why you're transitioning all of us from our previous details?" Train asked.

Andreas nodded.

"Our women are top priority for protecting, obviously. We've all got them covered. You're all part of the businesses. It's your money, investments and interest as well as all of the families. We've worked together for many years and have profited immensely. That will continue as long as we protect what is ours and do not allow any problems to push their way into our businesses and destroy them. No investigations by law enforcement and we'll be fine," Dominick stated.

"This may not be a situation. As we mentioned, it's rumor. Andreas, Cobra, and Sunny caught wind of it," Major said to them.

"Sunny, any inside information from your end?" Royce asked.

"No, and nothing underground or on the streets. I'm thinking this is high-end shit. Something that whomever is supplying it wants it kept quiet. We can't find shit," Sunny said to them.

"Do you really think it's a problem then for us?" Logic asked.

"It's a problem for the simple fact that we aren't running it or making money from it. Something so secretive could be deadly, and if bodies started to pop up then the cops would start sniffing around. As they push things and investigate then they uncover other shit. Shit we've kept lids on for years and are profitable. We need to be aware. This meeting is about awareness, and hopefully won't eventually turn into future meetings about elimination of product and dealers attempting to either move in on our territory or take advantage of our successes," Collin stated firmly.

"Whatever you need. We'll do what is necessary and put out feelers of our own. I think a good place to start would be our bartenders. They see and hear a lot," Ziek said to them.

"They also don't want to risk losing their jobs and pretend to not see or hear, just make and serve drinks," Rogan, Morano's guard, stated.

"It's precaution for now. Perhaps these little inquiries will be enough to keep whomever is dealing and whatever this shit is, out of our places so it won't become our problem," Morano said.

"Wouldn't that be nice and neat," Train mumbled and they chuckled.

The bosses ended the meeting and then the bullshitting began again.

"What was with those dicks messing with Alda the other night?" Morano asked Brew. The others stopped talking and Brew looked at Royce.

"Two of the guys were her cousins. The other two dicks are wannabes working with Mickey and Spence. They're losers, like bottom of the barrel shit," Brew told Morano.

"The two guys, you say are her cousins, they asked Derrick about jobs with us, and if we were hiring," Dominick said and the guys started laughing. Derrick worked with Andreas and was one hard ass security guy.

"What did Derrick tell them?" Logic asked.

"I think he laughed in their faces and told them that being mall cops better suited them," Morano said and they laughed.

"I noticed Alda left alone after you guys stepped in to save her from getting mauled by the two dicks," Ziek stated. Everyone got quiet and Royce stared at Ziek.

"Noticed Alessa left with someone, and it wasn't you, Ziek," he countered and the low "oohs" went through the room. It had become pretty fucking obvious who was interested in what women. The fact that Royce and his team now became the brunt of this type of teasing pushed him to take these feelings more seriously. It pissed him off. No woman was going to make him constantly think of her or want her. That gave a woman power and no woman ever had power over him.

"That's a guy she works with. He's got a girlfriend," Ziek added straight-faced. Royce could tell Ziek was getting pissed and Cobra, too.

"Well, maybe all of you can get your heads out of your asses and just claim the woman you want and move on already. This back and forth teasing is bullshit," Collin stated.

"Well, they'll all have plenty of more free time to make dates, and court the lucky lady they've chosen. Just don't go breaking their fucking hearts or treating them like trash or we'll be dealing with our women giving us shit. This is a family. We don't need controversy or other nonsense. Now get your minds on work and what needs to be done. We'll see everyone at Club Magique Friday night," Morano told them and everyone began to walk out of the room.

Royce looked at Brew, Logic, and Train. Could anything more than sex come from making moves on Alda? Did he want that? Have the patience for something more, or the desire? Royce didn't think so. He was not the commitment type or one to be empathetic and caring. Hell, he was a rotten bastard who would think nothing of fucking the woman and then never talking to her again. His heart was hard and cold. A life's worth of heartache, pain, and near death experiences, too many to keep count of. No room for flowers, romantic dinners and being gentle and passionate. Not for him anyway, but he wouldn't hold back the others if she was what they wanted. He glanced at Logic, Train, and then Brew. They were just as hard and cold-hearted as he was. Who was he kidding?

* * * *

Alda was sitting at her desk. It was a hell of a Monday morning. The office was buzzing with gossip over the visit from Antonio Sparks and the possibility of the company going international.

Multiple people tried to press her for information but she refused to say a word and merely told them that she knew as much as they did.

Alda glanced at the clock, now concerned even more that Lisa wasn't at work yet. Lisa told her that she had an emergency and would be late.

There was a knock at her door and as she looked up Haley was there. Alda's heart instantly began to race. The woman put her on edge because Alda never knew what side of her personality Haley would show. The calm easy-going side or the vicious pit bull side.

"Good morning, Alda."

"Good morning, Haley. How are you?"

Haley looked around the office and walked over to the bookshelf. She touched one of the ceramic cupcakes Alda had gotten as a birthday gift from Donata. She turned toward Alda and smiled.

"What did you think about Antonio?" she asked her, surprising Alda. It must have shown on Alda's face as Haley quickly continued talking.

"He's a very attractive man, wealthy, important, and very interested in the company. He has some great ideas, and although Max and I are concerned about getting too big too quickly, we're hoping that you and Antonio can come up with something together."

"Together? What do you mean?" Alda asked.

"I would like you to run negotiations with Antonio and the future international sales of our products through his exporting company. As I mentioned, Max and I don't want to explode and then wind up imploding, if you know what I mean. It has the ingredients for disaster."

"Don't you usually handle this aspect of the business, along with the CEOs and negotiators?" Alda asked.

"Yes we do, and I'm not giving you complete control and range here, I'm asking that you use your experience, your knowledge of the company and what we want to achieve here at MAX and see if we can agree on some sort of business terms with Antonio. I want a clear mind, not one opinionated by the desires of his products reaching the masses, and surely not one solely on hoping to make a lot of money and not break even or sink."

She was describing herself and Maxwell. Alda nodded and gave a soft smile.

"If it's a clear head you need then I am more than willing to assist. What is the plan of action?"

Haley smiled.

"Very good. Antonio's secretary, Belinda, will be contacting you to set up some sort of meeting, casual or more formal. Antonio loves the city and the city life. I expect he'll want to take you out. Just keep in mind that we want this to work out. That we aren't ready or willing to sell the company or shares in it to him. Please him, Alda. Everything else will fall into place."

Alda didn't care for the way she said to please him. Especially as the woman gazed over Alda's body. Maybe it just appeared that way and she was just checking out Alda's business suit dress? She was meeting with the sales department in fifteen minutes, discussing what areas of promotion had been most successful and deciding on where to budget the funds for promotional purposes. This would all change if they were going to come up with an international deal with Mr. Sparks.

"Keep me posted," Haley said then squinted at her. "Where is Lisa? She was supposed to finalize the artwork on the design you came up with."

"Oh, she had an emergency. I'm sure Benny will be up to see you shortly."

"Good. It's an excellent design. You are truly talented, Alda, and an asset to any company, anywhere," she said to her. Alda smiled as Haley walked out of the room, but then she thought about her comment. What the hell did that mean? Was she trying to say she may not have a job for that much longer?

She felt her belly ache. She gathered her files and spreadsheets for the meeting and then called Benny on her way out of the office. He didn't pick up.

"Gale, have you seen Benny?" Alda asked her as she walked past the front desks.

"Yes, he was on the phone in his office then he headed upstairs to meet with Haley."

"Okay, excellent. I'll be back after my meeting," she told her and then headed upstairs.

* * * *

Lisa tried calling Alda again. She was still in the damn meeting and she didn't know what to do. There was no way she would make it to work today. Lisa's sister Maggie had called her this morning after one of her roommates never came home Friday night. Then she got a call by police that Cindy was in the hospital after being found in an alleyway. Lisa paced the waiting area as her sister, her sister's roommate Annie, and Lisa waited to find out how Cindy wound up in the alleyway. As Cindy spoke with the nurses and the police, she believed that Cindy was drugged and more than likely raped. They needed descriptions of the men who were dancing with her and Cindy's sister and roommate couldn't remember what the men looked like. They were the only possible suspects because the two men were the last ones seen with Cindy.

Lisa felt sick to her stomach. Especially as the officers explained about how often this occurs, how a lot of women don't report it because they're embarrassed about not knowing what happened to them and getting into this type of situation. The police went on to explain about how hard it is to prosecute even if they found the men who did this because the victim had very little if any recollection of what occurred.

She looked at her sister Maggie. She was three years younger than her. This could have been her sister at that club who was drugged and sexually assaulted. Tears stung her eyes and they waited to see what the next steps were. Cindy was going to need their support and a lot of counseling. There was no way Lisa was making it in to work today. No way.

* * * *

Alda was shocked and she covered her mouth with her hand and felt the tears fill her eyes. Poor Cindy, Lisa's sister's roommate. How terrible of a thing to happen to her. Alda couldn't imagine being in such a situation. Years ago she and her friends talked about watching their drinks, and not accepting drinks from guys unless they were right there watching the drinks get poured. There were so many precautions she and her friends would take over the years and perhaps they needed to revisit those precautions and not take for granted the familiarity of the places. Alda also couldn't believe that it happened at Fairway. She was pretty sure that club was owned by the Coglonie men.

She told Lisa to take her time caring for her friend and let her know when she would be back to work.

Ending the call, Alda called Giada and let her know what happened as Alda gathered her things and started heading out of the office. It was a long day and she looked forward to a quiet evening at home. Giada was just as upset as she was and Giada said she was going to tell Dominick, Giuseppe, and Andreas what happened.

By the time Alda got off the commuter bus and onto the sidewalk a block from her apartment building she was feeling exhausted. Hauling her bag, attaché case, and a grocery bag with stuff to make grilled chicken, salad, and a little rice, she spotted the black SUV outside of her building. As she got closer the concerned feeling began to increase, and she stopped short the moment Royce and Train got out of the SUV. They looked at her and she slowly approached, squinting her eyes at them.

"We need to talk," Train stated. He and Royce were big men. Tall, over six feet with muscles and very stern, hard expressions. In fact, she wondered if the two men even knew how to smile. At all.

"What about?" she asked.

Train looked at the walkway to her apartment building.

"Inside. Let us help you with those," he said and reached for the grocery bag.

"Oh, thank you." She stared at him and then at Royce, who looked at her, gazing over her business suit, and then motioned with his hand for her to go inside. She instantly obeyed, started to walk and then paused and looked over her shoulder.

She reached into her purse as they stood behind her, towering over her. She pressed in the code then slid her key card. Train pulled the door open and they entered the lobby. It was small, but set up nicely with planters and some chairs to sit in. There was another security pad by the stairs leading up as well as a small hallway then the elevators. As the doors opened two guys, Jack and Paul, came out, smiled at her and then squinted at Train and Royce.

"Hi, Alda. Everything good?"

"Yes, of course. Going to Dooley's?"

"What do you think?" Jack asked and winked at her.

"Of course. I guess now we know why you keep declining our offers for you to join us. Have a good night," Paul said as he and Jack exited. She avoided Train and Royce's eyes. She had been avoiding Paul and Jack's invites for a while now, and always made excuses. She just wasn't attracted to them.

"Friends of yours?" Logic asked with an attitude.

"Not really. They live on the same floor as I do, that's all," she said and when they got to the fifth floor the doors opened and they followed her down the hall and around the corner. She unlocked her door and pushed it open, letting them inside. She walked ahead of

Train. It was a nice two bedroom apartment, and she had a decent view of the back garden area and park the kids from the school played in.

"You can put the bag in here," she said from the kitchen. It was an open floor plan. One large room containing a living room, kitchen and dining area that could fit six at a table. She pulled the chicken from the grocery bag and put it into the refrigerator then the vegetables, too. She folded up the bag, placed it into the closet and then washed her hands.

"Would you like something to drink?" she thought to ask the two men who stood there blocking her by the island in the kitchen. Even in high heels they towered over her, and she was nervous as could be. These were made men. Powerful, resourceful and their close proximity was making her feel claustrophobic.

"We're good. We came by because we heard about a woman who wound up in the hospital from Giada. She said you were friends with her," Royce said.

She shook her head. "I'm not friends with the woman who wound up in the hospital. You see, one of the women I work with, Lisa, she has a sister Maggie who shares an apartment with two other women, Cindy and Annie. Cindy was the one who wound up in the hospital. It's terrible," she said and looked at Royce wearing a black leather jacket and navy blue shirt underneath. His bold brown eyes were large and stood out, his cheekbones appeared carved from stone and he squinted at her as she turned away and looked at Train.

She went to move, to suggest they walk into the living room because she felt on edge having both men blocking her in the kitchen. Train tilted his head and let his eyes roam over her body.

"What do you know about what happened?"

"Why are you asking me?"

Royce moved behind her and she gasped and turned to see what he was doing and her hip hit the counter.

Train reached out and placed his hand on the counter. She turned again, leaning against the counter with her hands back against it.

"Are you afraid of us?" Royce asked.

She swallowed hard.

"No," she said but even she could tell her response sounded lame.

"Don't lie to us. Ever," Royce commanded.

Train inhaled as he leaned closer, as if he were sniffing her hair. He reached over and fixed her necklace. She tilted her chin up toward him, feeling heated, confused.

"Why are you here?" she asked.

Train removed his fingers, letting the gold necklace slide through his fingers.

Royce spoke, grabbing her attention. He placed a hand on the counter by her hip and looked down at her. His brown eyes were fierce and she couldn't look away from him. His other hand landed on her hips. She didn't gasp. She didn't want to show fear or intimidation.

"Giada gave us details about what went down with this woman, Cindy. Did the hospital say what kind of drugs were found in her system?" Royce asked her.

"No. They said it could be a few different ones. They didn't quite have an answer for Cindy's description of feeling like everything was slowing down around her, and then waking up in an alley not knowing where she was or being able to remember anything at all. She couldn't even remember the two men who were dancing with her. They're the ones the cops think put the stuff in her drink."

"So they think it was powder form? Something quickly dissolvable?" Train asked and she glanced at him.

"I don't know. It's scary to think there are men out there that would do such a thing. Her friends feel terrible for not noticing anything suspicious about the guys or even her disappearing. Apparently Cindy's hooked up with guys before and her friends figured she left with the guys."

Royce stared at her.

"There are bad people out there, Alda. Men who think the only way to snag a beautiful woman's attention is by drugging her and forcing her to be with them. This could be any form of date rape drug out there. The only thing that stands out and has our full attention is that this situation occurred at one of our clubs, and we've heard some rumors about some new drug being distributed at a high price and to select individuals. It may not be the same thing some guys gave this woman, but we needed to know more."

"We want to stop this shit from coming anywhere near our places and the women who regularly party at our clubs, and the families' clubs," Royce said to her.

"Of course. I hope the police can find these men, but from my understanding things like this happen a lot, and there isn't much they have to go by or concrete evidence either."

"How about a rape kit? I'm assuming they did one and maybe they could get some evidence that way?" Royce asked. She flinched. He sounded so cold, even talking about such a terrible crime. She stared at him, forced herself to be strong, unaffected by the thoughts of such cruelty a man could inflict on a woman.

"They did, but she was cleaned up thoroughly. Like completely sanitized, as if these men or one man knew what to do to avoid being caught. It didn't sound promising at all," she said to them.

Train cupped her cheek and made her look at him. His hand was huge and she couldn't help the intimidated feeling she had as he touched her. The man could break her with one hand. *Holy God, what the hell am I thinking?* She looked away, only for him to cup her cheek and clench her chin firmly. Was she stupid turning away from a man like him? One so powerful and capable? He was a made man. Shit.

"You promise us that you take precautions. Don't accept any drinks from any men you just met, or leave your drink unattended. If for some reason you suddenly feel funny, make a scene. Draw attention to yourself and the people with you. Understood?" Train ordered. His tone, his expression were firm, commanding like he was reprimanding her, yet his eyes went from her eyes to her lips and for some reason she wondered what it would be like to be kissed by him. A man so big, muscular, and scary, as well.

She needed to snap out of this. She wouldn't be some woman they could touch when they wanted, or beckon when they were in the mood for sex. That's the kind of reputations they had. No commitments, no real attachments to anyone and especially not a woman. They had sex and were done with them.

So how crazy was it that she could sort of, maybe, understand why the women threw themselves at these men and would take whatever they could get? Yikes. No, no, no, be smart, be unaffected.

"I know, Train. I don't even want to go out to Merchants Friday night but I promised some friends I would go."

"Donata and Alessa?" Royce asked. She felt a little jealous and hoped these two weren't interested in her friends. She glanced at Royce as Train released her chin.

"They might be there, but I'm actually meeting a few friends from an old job. We get together every few months or so and do dinner, drinks, and dancing. Anyway, I'll be careful and take precautions."

She went to move and Train gripped her hips, stepped in front of her and pressed her against the counter. She gasped, held on to his forearms and stared up at him, her head nearly to the top of her back, he was so tall. His eyes gazed over her top and she knew the blouse to her business suit probably gaped open.

"I'm serious, Alda. You need to be on guard at all times. Maybe not drink too much, not even to get a buzz." He reached up and stroked her jaw. Her lips parted and she held his gaze.

"I'm a big girl, Train. I can take care of myself just fine."

He clenched his teeth and narrowed his eyes at her. Apparently her reply wasn't what he wanted to hear.

He lowered down closer. "You think you can, but this shit, whatever it is, is bad stuff. It leaves you helpless, unable to fight back, or resist what's being done to you. A man or men could undress you, take turns…" He shook his head.

"Train," Royce stated firmly. Train looked at her lips again and squeezed her hip bone then looked over her breasts and into her eyes.

"You mind my orders. You be on guard and ready for anything at all times, Alda. Men would do crazy shit for a woman like you. Crazy shit."

Why did the man's words, his hold on her, his eyes, fuck, his everything make her panties wet, her heart race and her body need more of him?

"Promise me," he said and reached up and stroked her jaw.

"I promise," she said in such a husky, sexy voice she made herself blush. His eyes widened a moment and then he released his hold and stepped back.

"We hope your friend is okay and gets through this," Royce stated, eyed her over and then turned to walk away. She followed them on shaky legs and once again realized why women accepted whatever these men would give, even if it were just one night of sex.

Royce opened the door, his expression blank, eyes narrowed as usual. "Lock up when we leave," he ordered her. She squinted, feeling offended, like they thought she was stupid or incapable of being aware and taking safety precautions, even simple ones like locking her door. She didn't dare tell them about the guy who got into the building a year ago and forced a woman into her apartment down the hall, raped her and robbed her. It was scary to learn the details, but it eventually came out that Kelly had met this guy at a bar, didn't lock her door and the man had been watching her and eventually followed her home.

This was New York City. You needed to be street smart and people smart. Bad things happened all over the world. There were bad people everywhere, but in order to lower Alda's chances of becoming a victim, she knew she needed to be smart, stay aware, take precautions and expect the unexpected. This whole situation with Cindy, and the knowledge now that some new drug hit the streets and the nightclubs was a reminder that she and her friends had been lackadaisical. It was time to revamp and focus.

Train stared at her as he stood in her doorway.

"Mind my orders, Alda," he commanded and then walked away. She closed the door and locked it right away then looked out through the peephole. Both men had waited and watched to listen to see if she locked up and obeyed their orders. She was going to lock the door either way, buddy.

She exhaled, feeling annoyed. Did they really think she needed them to tell her to lock up? She was freaking twenty-five years old, living in the city all her life. She'd seen some crazy shit, hell, experienced some, too, and…

She stopped raging as she inhaled the scent of their colognes still lingering in her apartment. She looked toward the kitchen and recalled them standing there, so big and attractive, commanding, sexy, and oh no. She was attracted to these men. Not just Train and Royce but Brew and Logic, too. How could she be so stupid? Brew fucked women. Yup, she knew this. Knew a woman who had the pleasure of being his bed mate for the night and she carried on like crazy about his tattoos and his aggressive behavior, taking her from behind. She fantasized about Brew. How many other women got to screw each of these men and fantasized about them? Still wanted them, never mind the new ones who maybe even stalked these men. Shit! *Wake the frig up, Alda.*

How could she, Alda Ruffinno, a twenty-five-year-old overworked businesswoman who had two lovers in her life, compete with that? She couldn't. Hell, she wouldn't. She hardly dated because men were always after sex. She shook her head and growled. *Enough. I'm making dinner and relaxing.* This week was going to be insanely busy. She would need Friday night to unwind and relax. She had looked forward to seeing her old co-workers. No more thoughts of Royce and his crew. No more.

Alda headed into her bedroom to change before she would prepare some dinner, have a glass of wine and eat alone. As she thought about that her crazy mind began to nag her. She didn't have to be alone. She could have asked Train and Royce to stay for dinner. "Grrr. They are not good for me or my reputation. I won't be one of those women. No way, no how," she exclaimed and washed up before she headed into the kitchen. As more thoughts entered her mind about the men, she realized very quickly that she couldn't stop the thoughts. She was one of those women she bitched about earlier. She was fantasizing about Royce, Train, Logic, and Brew. Son of a bitch. She needed to get them out of her head, and quickly.

Chapter 4

Train Meander had always been a hard man who lived a hard life. He did a lot of crazy shit, especially in college. He came from crap. Grew up in a shitty neighborhood, had to learn fast to fight with his fists, his mouth and attitude to get anywhere. He was always big. He and Royce, Logic, and Brew met in foster care. Abigail James was their saving grace. His heart ached just thinking about her. She was a damn angel. She didn't need the aggravation they all put her through, that was for sure. Despite being taken care of, putting a roof over their heads and food in their bellies, they were still trouble-making men with strong spirits and so much to prove.

He narrowed his eyes and looked at his brothers. They were his brothers despite their different names, different parents and different stories of where they got free from. Once they got into Abigail's home, things started to change for each of them.

He shook his head and exhaled. He hadn't thought about his past, about the mistakes he made, even getting to go to college because of Abigail. The woman had money. She chose to live a simple life after losing her husband so young. They never had the chance to have kids of their own and taking in Train had helped her heal, but in reality saved his life. Fourteen and out of control until he was beaten to a pulp and left for dead. Abigail said she looked into his swollen eyes and she saw to his soul. She told him he was special, and that she was going to give him a second chance at life. That he was her miracle. She had been working in the hospital volunteering and was there when the paramedics brought him in. Alone, living on the streets. She worked magic, finding out who he was, how he didn't have parents who wanted him but instead gave him up.

He felt sick. Why the fuck was he thinking about this shit after all these years? He looked at the others. They each had their stories, their heartaches and him and Royce, hell, they were going to kill one another if it weren't for Abigail. Royce had his heavy shit too and boy, did the two of them get in and out of some trouble they thought Abigail didn't know about. He inhaled. Abigail would be proud of them now. Hell, she was proud when he graduated college, as did Royce, then Train and Brew, who fought it hard. They nearly lost him. Brew was in love with Cassie.

When she was assaulted one night at a party, Brew went crazy and fought the guy who sexually assaulted her. He beat him to a pulp, nearly killed him and two other friends of the guy. They pressed charges and he went to jail. Then Royce and Train found out that Cassie had been seeing the guy behind Brew's back, and that night had sex with multiple men. All lies, the woman betrayed Brew and he wound up serving time. It changed Brew that was for sure. It was also the main reason why the man never took women seriously, and focused on working out, taking care of business, and being a soldier for made men like the Coglonie.

They each fit in well here, Royce getting on with Giuseppe while in college. He slowly brought each of them in. Got them hired by Dominick and Andreas, who worked out and trained with Brew and Train. Logic thought his business mind and accounting specialties lay elsewhere, like in the professional business world, but he soon realized how boring that was, and how less profitable, too.

Train smirked and then took a drink from his water bottle. They all had been through so much, and their bond, their connection was special. It was like nothing else they ever had. They were family, and family stuck together. Family survived together, and were the only ones they could trust and let down their guard with.

As he watched his bosses, Giuseppe, Dominick and Andreas with their woman, Giada, he couldn't help but wonder if men so bad ass, so hardcore and powerful as the Coglonies could let one woman into their lives, their hearts, could he and his brothers do the same? Was it a stupid fucking thought? They screwed so many women, partied so much, hell, women lined up to be their next bedmates. How the hell would one woman have the capabilities of keeping all of them from straying and only wanting her? It made no fucking sense at all.

Alda popped into his head. What the hell would a woman so damn gorgeous, sexy, professional, and young, Jesus, twenty-five years old, want with men as fucked up as them and filled with baggage? They were gang members, thieves, scholars, businessmen, and eventually made men. They didn't trust anyone but one another. They never let their guard down to let people close and certainly not a woman. A woman's loins could be a man's weakness. Weakness was unacceptable. Being weak, accessible, made them targets and vulnerable to attack and ultimately death. This was the reality of the world they lived in. Every time they got a call, an order, they had to leave, ask no questions and just do what had to be done.

There was no room for a woman in their lives. Nor did they want one woman, and one woman only. They lived in a penthouse. They worked day and night, slept four hours if that a night. Women expected commitment, entertainment, and to be catered to. They weren't men like that. They weren't soft, empathetic, or tolerant of emotions and feelings.

He started feeling pissed off but his eyes went back to Andreas, Giuseppe and Dominick with Giada. He watched them and how the men acted around her. Giada made them different. She made them care, made them angry and also happy. They nearly lost her and he was right there for all of it. He saw Gisella and how she got to Collin and Fedarro. Then he thought about Fina. Jesus, the woman got to Russian heavies like Hadeon, Paulo, and Andriy.

He ran his fingers through his hair and started to feel overwhelmed with things he just wasn't used to feeling. What made it worse was Alda kept popping into his head. Train thought about her body, how sexy she was in everything she wore. That shoulder length brown hair all salon finished. Those green eyes filled with passion, care, intimidation and fear of him and his brothers. That fucking turned him on. The large breasts, the swell of her ass, her long, tanned thighs, and her intelligence. She was class, sophistication and beauty.

Abigail would love her.

Fuck!

He turned around and headed out of the room. Work. He would focus on work and trying to find out who the assholes were trying to bring this date rape drug into their clubs. Into all clubs around the city. The fucking assholes.

With that thought came thoughts of Alda going out to Merchant's Friday night. He and his brothers would be there. They'd watch over her. No one was going to get their hands on Alda to hurt her or drug her. She didn't need to know his concerns or that he would be watching. No one would know how he really felt. It was better this way. They couldn't give Alda what she deserved and needed. They just weren't capable of it. Never were, and never would be.

* * * *

Antonio Sparks listened to Alda Ruffinno's response to his ideas. She was classy, sexy, sophisticated. Tatum would want her if he laid eyes on her. He knew he would. Hell, Antonio was interested in getting to know her on a more intimate level. She was that sexy, and her body? Jesus, her fucking body was exceptional. Even in the very conservative dress she wore today he could tell she was well endowed, and in great physical condition. What he would do to have her by his side traveling back to the UK and abroad to other places.

"I think your ideas are creative, Alda, but I am interested in more than just the cosmetic line. I'd like to provide exporting for the full line."

"The full line? I'm a little confused, Antonio. Haley and Maxwell only indicated that you were interested in the cosmetic line that will be unveiled in a few weeks."

"Yes, I'm certain that was what they thought, however, after speaking with you and getting more insight into the company I'm very interested in the profit we all can make working together."

"If you're talking about some sort of merger, or a shared ownership in the company, I'm afraid you'll need to discuss that possibility with Haley and Maxwell. I can negotiate terms and ideas for the products and promotional aspects as well as distribution. I'm sorry if you were misled somehow," she said to him.

He reached over and covered her hand with his. Her green eyes widened.

"Alda, I'm a man of action, and purpose. When I see something I want, I go after it," he told her and she squinted at him.

"This company has greater potential than Haley and Maxwell are tapping into," he added, obviously noticing how his previous line shocked her.

He released her hand and she eased it back then placed it on her lap. She looked a little uneasy. Had she felt the attraction too? God, this could be complicated. Once Tatum laid eyes on Alda it could be disastrous. The poor woman wouldn't know what hit her.

"They don't want to sell the company though."

He tilted his head sideways.

"Is this a personal fear or are you really concerned for what is best for MAX Industries?" he asked her. Her eyes widened as if shocked by his accusation but Haley did say she wanted to know where Alda's loyalties lay. It seemed Haley had plans for Alda, as well.

"To be honest with you, I've already worked for a few companies that decided to sell out instead of hold on and ride it. I've lost several jobs over things like this, however, it's all worked out so far. If Haley and Maxwell decided they wanted to sell the company to you so you can take it to the next level and go international, it wouldn't shock me at all. However, after speaking with both of them, they seem dead set on riding this out and making the company grow, but at their own speed, so they don't lose control and screw it up. I respect that, and maybe you should, too."

He was shocked at her gall, her dedication and loyalty to the company. Haley would probably be shocked, too. Not enough to not throw Alda to the wolves, or in this case, wolf. Tatum was going to love her. Maybe he would share. This was a first for Antonio, too.

"I respect your loyalty to the company and to Maxwell and Haley. In all honesty, do you think they might consider a partnership with me? I can see MAX Industries going to great heights with the right people working in the company. I could be a great asset to them, to you, Alda," he said to her.

He watched her swallow and then she gave a soft smile.

"I suppose your next meeting should be with them then." She reached out to take a sip of wine from her glass when her eyes landed on something behind him. She quickly looked back toward Antonio. He looked over his shoulder and saw several men walking into Rinaldi's and being greeted by the owner. The Coglonie family. Lou Carvetti warned him about them and the Fiorre family and their involvement in organized crime and their roles over business affairs in the city. Tatum wanted to ease back on the drug he was introducing here in the city. It was a very potent, unique drug that Tatum would not allow to be distributed freely. It was the drug of the wealthy and prominent. Only select amounts were distributed and for a hefty price.

"Men you know?" he asked her. Then took a sip from his glass of wine.

"Acquaintances of friends of mine, actually," she replied.

"You know some interesting individuals, Alda. It surprises me," he said to her, holding her gaze.

"Why is that?" she asked.

"You're so sweet, and seem…vanilla," he said, surprising her. He couldn't get over how flirty he felt. The woman definitely intrigued him. Her face flushed and it brought that attraction up a notch. She wasn't experienced with men. Oh, this was getting even better than expected.

She glanced at him, unsure of how to respond. He leaned closer.

"I've shocked you? I apologize. I know I'm older, a bit more seasoned in a lot of areas," he said and let his gaze slide over her features, and her breasts. Her cheeks blushed again. He was getting to her.

"I think you should remember this is business, Antonio."

"I didn't intend to offend you, Alda, but to compliment you."

"Really?" she challenged. His arousal grew.

"Definitely compliment you. You're a very attractive woman. You're professional, classy, and your eyes are stunning. You are the whole package, and definitely a good prospect for the idea Haley and I discussed. I wasn't so sure at first, but now I'm thinking you would fit the part."

"You've lost me, Antonio," she said, and her eyes gazed back toward the men as they headed into the bar area. She gave a wave and a smile and as Antonio looked he saw a few very large men nod their heads at her but they weren't smiling. They looked lethal. Nothing a bullet couldn't get rid of. He cleared his head.

"As I was saying, Haley and I were throwing around some ideas before I headed out here with my partner."

"Partner?" she asked.

"Yes, he's more like a silent partner, and doesn't really like crowds, or to have to handle the social aspect of business. He's great with numbers. A workaholic, but I'm certain he will love meeting you eventually. That's if this all works out."

"Do explain what you mean. Haley hasn't mentioned any of this."

"We were brainstorming when we met months ago in Rome. I have a villa there. So stunning and relaxing. Perhaps if all goes well you'll get to visit." She narrowed her eyes at him.

"I'm jumping the gun. I haven't even explained the idea. I shouldn't have brought it up. Haley will be angry with me. It's just some preliminary ideas. I am surprised though that she hadn't mentioned any of this."

"Haley likes to keep things under wraps until she's a hundred percent certain it will go off as she expected."

"I can give you a little information now. You see, with this new cosmetics line we had the idea of having a symbol, an image and person to associate with the label that you created. Haley wants someone with the right look, the right demeanor and also something different. A person involved with the company and its wellbeing. She thought of you, Alda."

"What do you mean?" she asked.

He leaned back and eyed her over.

"You as the face, the representation of MAX Products."

Her eyes widened, her jaw dropped and she blinked several times. She was precious. He chuckled.

"Take a sip of wine," he said to her and she did. Even that aroused him. She would take orders well. She would fit both his and Tatum's needs and desires. Holy shit. This was quite unexpected indeed.

* * * *

"Is that the same rich prick from the other night with Alda?" Ziek asked Brew and Logic.

"How would we know?" Logic asked, but took a seat by the end of the bar where he could glance back to see Alda. Logic wondered who the guy she was with was. He was older. Had a distinguished look about him. Wore a fancy suit, and Logic could see the fucker's gold and diamond cuff links from here. The silly prick. His chest tightened and his gut reacted. He was fucking jealous.

"You guys should make a damn move already if you're that interested in her. She's gorgeous. Shouldn't be single," Ziek added and took a sip from his glass of brandy.

"We've been over this, Ziek. Same shit with you and your buddies making a move on Alessa. Not commitment type of guys."

"Then don't look so fucking pissed off," Ziek countered.

"That coming from the guy who was about to go over and tear a guy away from Alessa the other night when the guy kissed her and she pushed him away?" Logic added. Ziek snorted and they chuckled. Brew wasn't saying a word.

"What the fuck is wrong with us?" Ziek asked.

"We're not good men when it comes to women. Just not the nurturing kind," Logic said and then clenched his teeth.

"They're getting up from the table and making their way to the bar. You know the dick wants in her panties," Brew said.

"Of course he does. They're dining at Rinaldi's," Ziek said, just as a few women they knew came over to join them and flirt. Logic looked over the brunette in the tight red dress and too much makeup. She was attractive, had a nice set on her but he wasn't in the mood. Nor was Brew as some redhead smoothed her hand over his shoulder and whispered hello to him. Brew's angry expression and nonverbal response didn't stop the redhead from touching his brother. Brew's eyes were on Alda and the guy she was with as they entered the bar area. The brunette took that moment to place her hand on Logic's shoulder and caress him then whisper to him. Logic caught Alda's eyes. She was pissed, hell, jealous maybe and his gut clenched. He pressed the brunette away only it was too late. Alda passed them with her date, and went to the end of the bar, her back toward them.

He stared at her, and the older man who towered over Alda. The bar was crowded, but he had a good line of sight on her backside. As people pressed closer, the dick took the opportunity to slide his hand along her waist, nearly to her full, round ass.

"You look about ready to explode," Ziek said to him and then turned to look.

"What is it?" Brew asked.

"Nothing," Logic said. He didn't know how Brew would react. Alda wasn't even their woman, or a woman they fucked, yet they were jealous of other men paying attention to her and flirting with her.

"Want me to find out who he is?" Ziek asked.

"No," Logic said.

"Hey, you'd do it for me. You guys are into her. I've never seen any of you into one woman and one woman only. You haven't even hooked up with any women, and you just got rid of two easy, sexy fine specimens of women just now and that was why we came out tonight," Ziek stated.

"I guess we weren't in the mood," Brew said and then took a sip from his beer.

"The guy is stepping away. Looks like he got a phone call. I'll go talk to her and say hello," Ziek said.

Logic grabbed his arm. "I'll go," he said and looked at Brew. No response. No reaction. He was on his own.

The guy walked to the hallway and Alda stood there alone. As Logic approached some other guy started to head toward her and Logic got to her. Alda's eyes landed on the guy and then on Logic.

"Take a hike," he told the guy and the guy immediately turned around and left.

Her lips parted, her green eyes landed on him and he took in the sight of her. Holy fucking shit, did she look gorgeous in this lighting. Her green eyes sparkled, her lips looked full and lush, her cheeks pink and the dress she wore hugged her figure so tight he could see every bit of her curves. The wrap style dress looked like one yank on the side would make the whole thing come undone.

"How are you, Alda?" he asked her and placed his beer down on the bar. She looked toward the hallway, as if checking to see if her date was coming back.

"Good. How are you, Logic?"

"Good. Who's the guy?" he blurted out and she squinted at him.

"Excuse me?" she asked.

He exhaled. He didn't mean to be so blunt or to make it obvious that the sight of her with another man pissed him off.

"The guy you're with. I've never seen him before. Wanted to make sure that you were okay," he added.

Her expression immediately changed and she looked annoyed. She rolled her eyes and looked away then took a sip of her wine. "I'm a big girl, Logic. I told Train and Royce that the other night. I don't need you looking after me like some big brother," she snapped.

"Big brother?" he asked. Jesus, the woman didn't know how fucking hot she was. Fired up, she was even hotter and his thoughts were not one from a big brother's perspective.

He stepped closer and placed his hand on her hip. "I don't want to be your fucking big brother," he said to her and held her gaze.

She looked at him as if trying to read him and his words. He couldn't believe this. It was getting harder and harder to not want this woman in his arms, in his bed with his cock buried deep in her cunt. Holy fuck, he felt desperate.

"Everything good, Antonio?" she asked and looked toward the right as her date approached. He removed his hand from her hip and looked the guy over. He was an inch taller than Logic, very well groomed with his hair slicked back and the dusting of gray making him appear distinguished. He narrowed his eyes at Logic as if unimpressed with him. The man didn't know who the fuck Logic was.

The guy stepped closer to Alda and slid his arm against her back to the bar.

"Are you okay?" he asked her, holding her gaze and staring at her lips.

Alda stared right back up at the guy. "Of course. This is Logic, a friend of mine," she said and introduced him.

She turned to look at Logic.

"Logic, meet Antonio Sparks," she said. Antonio reached out his hand to shake Logic's and when he did the guy gripped it hard. Logic gripped it harder, their eyes narrowed.

"Is everything okay, Antonio? Was the call important?" she asked as Antonio released Logic's hand. The man was fucking challenging him over Alda. *I don't think so, dick.*

"Unfortunately I need to head out. On the way, my driver can drop you off at your place," he said to her. So the dick had a driver. He wasn't the driver like Logic and his brothers had been for their bosses. Although that was somewhat behind them with their new roles maybe Alda saw them as lesser men. What the hell was she thinking? They were loaded, bad ass powerful enforcers, not chauffeurs. Fuck. They protected their bosses with firearms and physical capabilities this dick in his designer suit didn't have.

"Oh, that's okay. No need for that. I was going to catch a cab or the subway home anyway," she replied.

"You're not taking the subway home this time of night," Logic chimed in.

"Excuse me," Antonio said and then took her hand and pulled her a few feet away. Logic couldn't hear the conversation. When he saw Antonio pull her close, whisper into her ear and let his hand slide down her back to nearly her ass, he felt sick, angry, but then Alda reached back and stopped him. She wasn't into the guy. Thank God.

He kissed her cheek goodnight.

"You're sure."

"Yes. I am. I'll speak to you over the weekend," she said to him.

"We'll get together. Something nice. Just the two of us," he said and then eyed over Logic.

What an asshole.

Antonio left and Alda stepped back toward the bar.

"Guess the call was important," he said to her.

"I guess so," she said and took a sip from her wine.

"His loss, my gain," he said to her and reached out and pushed a strand of hair from her cheek.

"Don't think so, Logic. Maybe you should head back over to where your friends are so you can be with those women I saw all over you as I walked in here." She went to move and Logic just stared at her as Brew came up at that moment and placed his hand on her waist and slid in next to her.

"Alda," he said, and leaned down and kissed her cheek. She didn't turn away, instead she tilted her head up toward Brew and accepted his kiss.

"Brew," she said his name and Brew slid his arm along her waist but Alda stepped back and leaned against the bar. She looked at Logic and gave him an annoyed expression.

"I was just talking Alda into staying here and having a drink with us since her date had to leave early," Logic said to Brew.

"Great, another glass of wine?" Brew asked.

"I think I'm done," she said to him.

Brew stared down at her lips and then over her body. Logic hid his grin.

"No, you're not done. You'll have a drink with us," he told her and she looked intimidated, yet her cheeks went flush.

She was silent and Logic watched her closely. Brew handed her a glass of red wine and then lifted his glass of brandy toward her.

"To your date leaving you here with us," Brew toasted and held her gaze.

"He didn't leave me," she said to him.

"Sure he did. That's why you're here with us," Logic stated, stepping closer. They were both caging her in and she looked affected, like he felt.

"Something came up that was important," she countered.

Brew stroked her hip. "If you were out on a date with me, nothing would tear me away from you, Alda," he said, shocking Logic. Alda laughed and then took a sip from her wine glass. Brew chuckled and then took a sip.

"Lines like that actually work for you, Brew?" she asked, smirking.

"When my good looks and amazing personality butter them up first," he said to her. She laughed again, and smiled, the sound affecting Logic's heart. Holy shit, this was different.

"What, you don't believe me?" Brew asked.

"Oh, I believe you. I've heard stories, too, and remember when I walked in and you had a couple of women throwing themselves at both of you and Ziek, too. I guess in your line of work it rains women," she said and took a sip from her glass as if bored with the subject. Was she insulting them, jealous, uninterested? She couldn't be. He was so damn attracted to her and so were his brothers. This had to be different, and real.

"As I assume in your line of work it rains rich, snobby men looking to land an intelligent, sexy, model with body and brains," Brew told her and she stared at Brew.

"Model? I think not, but nice try again. Brains? Definitely, which is why as soon as I'm finished with this glass of wine, I'm heading home," she told Brew.

"Not alone," Logic added. She looked at him.

"You too now, Logic? Hmm, I suppose the whole tag team thing probably works on most women you associate with. Not me, though. Remember, I've been around you guys for months. I've seen you in action." She took a sip from her glass of wine.

Brew slid his hand along her belly and Logic stroked her chin.

"I don't think you've seen us in action, Alda. You've seen us getting through life, accepting who we are and what we deserve," Logic said to her and she held his gaze.

Logic moved his mouth closer to her lips and she turned just as his lips touched her cheek.

"Invite us to come home with you," Brew said to her as she turned and his lips covered Alda's. Logic pulled back, his body completely aroused like nothing he ever felt before as he watched Brew kiss Alda. He slid his hand under her hair and kissed her deeply then slowly released her lips and pulled her against his chest.

"Let's go," he said to her and Alda gripped his arms, pulled back and stared at Brew then looked at Logic. Her lips were full, lush and inviting. He wanted to taste her, too. Hell, he wanted to strip her from this dress and fuck her until she was out of his head. Obviously Brew wanted that, too.

"I don't think so, Brew. Remember what I said about knowing you guys so well." Brew looked at her face, her lips as he remained holding her. She pressed from his embrace.

"I also know women you and your buddies have used. Hell, have screwed. I won't be just some other woman you've gotten to spread her legs. I deserve better than that. I've got more class, more respect for myself than that, no matter how good those kisses of yours may feel," she said and reached up and stroked his jaw.

Brew gripped her wrist tight. "You playing games with us?"

"No, Brew. You're the one who is into games. Into no commitments, and not taking any woman and emotions seriously. I get it. It's your life and your buddies' lives."

"You feel the attraction, Alda. To all of us," Logic stated firmly. She looked at him and clutched her purse.

"Yes, I do, but you're all wrong for me. I don't sleep around, and all of you do. I don't play games, but you see every woman as a game, as a challenge to get her into bed. Do you seriously insult me and put me into the same category as those women? Good night, and thanks for the drink," she said and walked away from them.

Logic was shocked, but Brew looked even more perplexed. He grabbed his drink and finished it. He stared straight ahead at the bar and Logic did the same, not saying a word for some time.

"She thinks we're a bunch of male whores," Brew stated some time later, his mind obviously going over what happened as well as what he'd done with his life. Logic was doing the same thing.

"She sees us for what we are, Brew. Enforcers, soldiers, made men for the Coglonie family. We fuck people up, we take care of business, we've had shitty lives up to the point where we got involved with this life."

"Women are all the same. They're after something. She's no different," Brew said, spitting his venom which was so Brew. He fought emotions. Hadn't been trusting since Cassie years ago and serving time for assault. Logic couldn't blame him. Their childhoods sucked until Abigail.

"I don't think so, Brew. I actually liked that she told us what she was feeling and was straight up with her impression of us. She admitted to the attraction. It's our inability to show any desire to commit to one woman, and date. She's right. We've never dated a woman. Hell, we've used them for our needs and not even that often," Logic stated.

"Speak for yourself," Brew said and Logic chuckled.

"So you're offended by the truth? By the fact that she knows women who you screwed and it makes her jealous and pissed off, and untrusting?"

"Fuck yeah."

"Well, put the shoe on the other foot, bro. Doesn't the thought of another man fucking her drive you insane? Make you want to lose your shit?"

"Been there, done that, and served my time because of it. In the end, what did I find out? It was all a fucking game. How do we know Alda isn't full of shit?"

"We've been around her for a while now. We know her friends and none of them are whores looking to land a guy or guys. In fact, they each fought their attractions."

"This is different, Logic. We don't do commitments. We don't trust anyone but one another. We've never dated, or played that whole scene. We live dangerous lives and have hurt people with our bare hands. These hands can't be gentle. Our hearts are so hardened there's no way we can be empathetic or care for one woman and one woman only like that."

"Then why the hell do I feel this emptiness now that Alda walked away from us? Answer me that? Where the fuck are these feelings coming from? Why did I care so much seeing her with that dick she was with? Why are Royce and Train concerned for her too and why the fuck did you kiss her?"

Brew was silent a moment and then he spoke.

"To try and get her out of my head. If I have her, maybe I could walk away."

"From her? Never going to happen. I think we all realize that and it scares the fuck out of us. She's gorgeous, and that body, those eyes, the way it feels when she's close. It's all different, Brew. Fucking different."

"Well, different isn't good. Different causes problems. We got a good life, a good way of handling things. We don't ever have to be lonely."

"Sex is temporary satisfaction, Brew. It sure the fuck doesn't fill the gap. Not by a long shot," Logic said then slugged down the remainder of beer and twirled his finger for another round. He was going to need lots of alcohol tonight to numb this feeling.

* * * *

"What do you want us to do?" Matt asked Antonio.

"Get her cleaned up and out of there. Dope her up more and then dump her. How is Tatum?"

"Raging. If we didn't come into the room he could have killed her."

"What the fuck happened? How did this happen?"

"He took something, Antonio. Something new, he said."

"Fucking moron. I'll be there in thirty minutes to deal with him. Get the others and make sure nothing is left on her for anyone to figure shit out."

"We will. We'll be extra careful."

"Good."

Antonio disconnected the call and looked out the window as his driver headed to New Jersey. He was so pissed off that he had to leave Alda. Now he wondered if he should even let Tatum see her. Why the fuck did he take drugs? What the hell was Tatum thinking? Fuck!

Chapter 5

Alda completely ignored Brew, Logic, Train, and Royce since she arrived with old co-workers over an hour ago. She was dancing with them now, laughing and having a good time even as some guys joined them on the dance floor. Donata and Alessa were there too and talking to a couple of guys when Alda decided to head off the dance floor and get a drink. She walked over toward the bar, and some guy was watching her. A big guy, who looked a little drunk. She slid her hands along the deep green dress she wore. It had one shoulder showing and the other had one strap and the shoulder covered. It was sexy but comfortable.

A few seconds later Alessa joined her at the bar.

"I love this dress on you. You got it at Milly's boutique, you said," Alessa asked her.

"Yes, I did. I love that store. I'm going back this week. The owner said they're having a sale so I'm sure they'll be a bunch of spring things out," Alda said to her.

"Maybe we can go together. I need a few new dresses. My cousin Joanie is getting married in few months and it's in South Carolina so I want something sexy and totally New York style."

"I'm sure you'll find something amazing. Does she know her colors yet?" Alda asked just as some guy bumped into the back of her. As she turned there were a few men there talking and then the one big guy placed his hand on Alda's hip.

"Hey, gorgeous, come on out and dance with me," he said to her and pulled her close. She grabbed on to his arm.

"I don't think so, buddy. Let go," she said to him.

"She doesn't want to dance," Alessa said, stepping away from the bar. It was crowded there.

"I think she does. She fits perfectly in my arms," the guy said and Alda felt his hand squeeze her ass.

"Hey," she yelled and then shoved at him.

"Let her be. She's having a drink and then she'll dance later maybe," some guy said to him and as the guy released her Brew slammed his hand on the guy's shoulder.

"There a problem over here, Alda?" Brew asked, looking so angry it scared Alda. She thought he might kill the guy.

Alda touched Brew's arm, felt the thick, hard muscles under his sleeve. "It's okay, Brew, he's leaving now. It's fine."

"It didn't look fine," Brew stated firmly.

The big guy looked at the other guys behind Alda and near Alessa and the bar.

"My mistake, man. Sorry," he said to Alda and she nodded.

Brew released him and then looked over Alda. "You okay?" he asked.

"I'm fine, Brew." He moved closer to her, wrapped his arm around her waist and walked her back closer to Alessa.

"They come back over or you have any problems, make a scene," he ordered. She nodded. He slid his hand away from her body and walked away.

"Holy crap, Brew was going to tear that guy a new one. What the hell?" Alessa asked Alda as she reached back to the bar to take a sip of her drink.

"I know, that was scary. He was so pissed off."

"Well, you have been ignoring them all night."

"Alessa, I told you why."

"Yeah and I think you're crazy. Brew kissed you."

"He was after a good time."

"No, it's more than that."

"Oh really. Maybe you should take your own advice and let Lenox, Cobra, Roman, and Ziek take you to bed," Alda challenged and Alessa rolled her eyes.

"They don't exactly fit into my family's ideas of the perfect relationship for me. A ménage, no less? I'm on bad terms with the family as is. The only reason why I got invited to the wedding is because my cousin and I remained close."

"Isn't she marrying two guys?"

"Yup. That was a shocker for the Preston family."

"I'm sure not as much of a shocker as you leaving law school to go to baking school," Alda teased.

"Are you two ladies okay?" a guy that was dancing with Alessa earlier asked. Alessa pushed her hair behind her ear and smiled.

"Yes. Thank you."

"Guys can be such assholes," he said to her.

"Yes, they can," Alessa stated and then Alda looked away and toward the bar across the room where she saw Brew, Royce, Lenox, Cobra, and Harley standing. A lot of the guys were there tonight. She then looked away so they wouldn't think she was checking them out or anything. On the dance floor Donata and the girls were having fun and Alda excused herself to go back out there. Alessa was enjoying a conversation with the guy and gave her a thumbs up. Alda walked away and the other guy took her place by the bar.

As she danced and enjoyed the music with her friends she thought about Brew's reaction and how quickly he got to her. That meant he had been watching her and she couldn't help but feel giddy about it. She ignored the attraction, not wanting any of the problems that would come along with it. A few times she glanced back toward the bar and now Alessa and the guy who was with her were walking toward the side hallway. She noticed Alessa lose her footing and the guy grabbed her around the waist. Her gut clenched. Something wasn't right. She hurried through the crowd, pushing by people just trying to get to her friend. As she got to her right before the side exit door she knew her gut was right.

"Hey." She grabbed on to the guy's shoulder and Alessa looked drunk. She went to hold her. "What's going on?"

"Oh, your friend is a little tipsy. We were going to go outside for some fresh air. I got her. Don't worry," he said and the guy pulled Alessa close against his side.

"Alessa, are you okay?" she asked her.

"No. Something is wrong," she said.

"Nothing is wrong. She'll be fine with fresh air." He pulled her along and Alda grabbed on to the guy.

"No. Something is wrong. What did you do?" she yelled and then shoved at the guy. She remembered Train and Royce's advice about making a scene.

"Let go of her. Help!" Alda screamed. The guy shoved at her and tried to pull Alessa to the exit.

"What's going on?" Donata asked and two of the other women approached, too.

"He's trying to take her. He gave her something," Alda said as Donata and the girls pulled Alessa into their arms. The guy pulled out a knife.

"Stop right there!" Alda turned and saw Brew, Royce, Lenox, Ziek and others coming to help and the guy grabbed Alda around her waist and pulled her backward. He had the knife against her neck. Brew, Royce, and the men all looked fierce.

"Let her go, man. Right the fuck now!" Brew yelled and stepped forward.

"No. I'll cut her," he yelled, backing up. Alda was shaking and looking at the men and her friends and then Alessa passed out.

"Alessa!" Alda screamed just as someone came up behind the guy with a gun or something and as he released her the blade cut her dress and skin on the side. She covered it with her hand as Royce pulled her into his arms and Logic decked the guy. In a flash they were moving him out of the club and down the hallway.

Royce hugged her and Brew pressed up against her back.

"You're okay, baby. You're okay. You did the right thing and yelled for help," Royce said to her. She lifted her chin up, felt the tears roll down her cheeks then looked at Alessa. Cobra was carrying her through the crowd.

"Alessa? Is she going to be okay?" she asked.

"Come on. We'll all go upstairs and get to the bottom of this."

"The guy?" she asked and looked over her shoulder.

Brew had a hand on her hip. "Harley, Roman, and Ziek will find out everything. You're safe. That's what's important," Brew said and kissed her shoulder.

She went to walk, her legs shaking, she was so shocked at what happened. She looked down at her side. Her hand had a little blood on it.

"He cut you?" Royce yelled.

"What?" Brew asked. She saw their expressions and then saw Logic and Train coming over.

"Royce?" Logic asked.

"He cut her. Let's get her upstairs. Are Harley and the guys handling the asshole?"

"Yes," Train said and eyed over Alda. A moment later, with her eyes glued to Royce's fierce ones, her heart hammering inside of her chest and too many emotions going through her body, he lifted her up and carried her through the crowd and upstairs.

* * * *

Royce was fuming, fucking mad. One look at his brothers, their angry expressions and their concern and nothing else seemed to matter but keeping Alda close and protecting her. His heart was pounding inside of his chest and as the doors opened there was still chaos going on over Alessa. They walked into the room and Alessa was definitely on something.

"What the fuck did he give her?" Brew asked.

"We don't know. Harley and the guys will find out. Then we'll take it from there," Cobra stated.

"Should we call the police?" Donata asked.

"Not yet. We need to find out what this dick gave her, then maybe find out where he got the shit," Cobra said to her.

"What for? You caught the guy. Let him get in trouble for doing this to her."

"Donata, remember that girl I told you about and her friend who wound up in the hospital?" Alda asked. Brew and Train were looking at the cut on her side.

"Yeah. You think this is connected?" Donata asked.

"We don't know but if we can find out what it is and where it's coming from then maybe we can stop it from spreading and get the ones responsible arrested," Logic told her.

"We need to see how deep this is. Come on," Train said to her. Alda looked at Alessa and Donata and she was worried about her friend. She knew that Cobra and the team would take good care of her so she let Train take her hand as he, Brew, Royce, and Logic brought her into the other room.

* * * *

Train gripped her hips and stared down into her eyes. He reached up and cupped her cheek.

"Okay?" he asked her and the tears fell. He pulled her into his arms and hugged her. When she hugged him back he exhaled, relieved that she didn't push them away. After hearing about what she said to Brew, he didn't think they stood a chance with her. He'd been fighting this attraction, as well, but every time he saw her with another guy, it pissed him off. Then when she was in danger tonight it sent him into a rage. Thank God their friends took care of questioning the dick that drugged Alessa and hurt Alda. He wouldn't have kept the dick alive once he got what he needed from him.

He pulled back.

"We need to unzip the dress and see the damage. If it's deep and you need stitches then we'll need to make a decision as to what to do."

"I understand. You'll want to question the guy to see what information you can get from him, and then pull all your stories together if the police need to come."

"Exactly, Alda," he told her.

She looked down. "I don't think it's bad. If you give me the first aid kit and direct me to a bathroom I could probably…"

He shook his head no and she stopped talking.

Royce moved in behind her.

She held on to Train's forearms as the zipper went down. The moment her breasts came into view, pouring from the matching silk bra, he lost his breath. Then came the tattoo on her hip bone below the knife wound and then the belly ring and her sexy hips. Behind her Royce exhaled and locked gazes with Train. Logic lowered down by her side and slid his palm along her lower back to her hip.

"Sweet heavens, woman," Logic said and she looked down at him.

"This isn't a smart idea," she whispered.

Train slid his palm up her arm to her shoulder and under her hair against her neck. He tilted her head up toward him.

"Trust us to take care of you, and not hurt you."

She exhaled a laugh then squinted at him.

"Seriously?" she asked, her voice cracking.

She jerked as Logic began to clean up the cut and Brew stood watching, holding the kit in his hand, his eyes on her body.

"You don't need stitches, baby," Logic said to her and she went to look at him but Train gripped her chin and jaw more firmly.

"That could have been you they drugged. You, that piece of shit attempted to take out of here. No one would have seen a thing. We could have kept ignoring these feelings we have for you and you for us, and acted pissed off and kept our eyes off of you. Instead we couldn't keep our eyes off of you, because you're so fucking perfect. So sexy, classy and gorgeous. This has to fucking end, Alda."

"Train." She said his name and began to shake her head but Train covered her mouth, kissing her. Logic had already placed ointment on the cut and covered it when Train pulled her close, ran a hand along her ass, squeezing her to him. He cupped her breast as she moaned into his mouth. Then Royce gripped her hair where Train was holding her and he suckled against her neck. She tightened up but then rocked her hips against Train, feeling aroused by both of them touching her, kissing her.

"Holy fuck. Do you guys feel it?" Logic asked.

"It can't be real," Brew said to the side of them.

"It's real. It's fucking incredible," Royce said, lifting from suckling her neck. Slowly Train released her lips. He stared into her wide eyes, saw her stunned expression.

"Things are going to fucking change, Alda. You understand me? Change," he ordered. Then there was a knock at the door and he pulled her close. Brew went to answer it.

"We'll be down shortly," Brew said then closed the door.

"What did they say?" Logic asked.

"You know Harley. He's got a way of making people talk and give up information quickly. They need us."

Train reached down and stroked her jaw.

Royce kissed her neck from behind her and she closed her eyes and leaned back against him, feeling the attraction.

"You stay upstairs with Alessa while we handle this situation. Understood?" he asked.

"Yes, Royce," she said and he eased her dress back into place.

Then Logic fixed the material and pressed close, kissing her. "Do not leave that office," he ordered. She nodded. He slid his hand along her ass and they walked her into the other room where Alessa lay on the couch completely sedated. One look at Cobra and Lenox and Train knew they were pissed.

"Look at her. She wouldn't know or feel a thing right now. I could undress her, place her where I want to…fuck!" he yelled out and Alda jumped, grabbing on to Train's waist.

"We got to her in time. She's safe with us," Royce said, sliding by Alda and bringing her hand to his lips. He kissed it.

"Alda, you saved her. That guy would have taken her out of there. We couldn't even see you guys where we were standing," Lenox said to her.

"We all were there. We saved her together," Alda stated.

"How is the cut? Need stitches?" Cobra asked her.

"No. She'll be okay," Train said and squeezed her to his side.

Alda stepped from his hold and Royce's and knelt down next to Alessa. When she turned around to look at them she had tears in her eyes.

"Find out who these people are and where this drug is coming from, and stop them. Please," she said. A tear fell and she wiped it away and then caressed her friend's hand.

They all headed out of the room, leaving Alda, Alessa, Cobra, Lenox and Donata in the room together.

* * * *

"I don't know who the supplier is. I got it from a dealer. I had to pay five hundred bucks for one fucking pill," the guy yelled at them. Brew slugged him in the mouth again.

"We want a name. A number and location," Harley demanded.

"They'll kill me. The guy that hooked me up said they only distribute fifty of these pills a week."

"Fifty?" Harley yelled through clenched teeth.

Brew was raging. He couldn't believe the shit he was hearing. That's how many poor unsuspecting females would be loaded up on this drug and unaware of what was being done to them. Scumbags.

Brew pulled out his revolver and pressed it against the guy's temple. The guy screamed out in a high pitched tone. "You think I'm not going to fucking kill you, asshole? You got five fucking seconds to tell me where you got the shit. The number you called, who hooked you up and what your fucking plans were."

As the guy rambled off numbers and a name then a location Brew was getting more pissed off. Then he explained that he was bringing Alessa to a house where there was a party of guys who chipped in for the thousand dollars to get two women. That Alda was the second one. He called her the sexy brunette with the green eyes. Brew felt sick.

Before he could even react in anger, Roman decked the guy and knocked him onto the floor. Brew realized in that moment how much Roman cared about Alessa. It also made Brew see that these feelings he had for Alda were real and not bullshit. It really could have been Alda drugged up too right now. Obviously she didn't drink that drink by the bar.

Back upstairs as she stood there practically naked, looking like some sexual fantasy come true, and his brothers kissed her, and they surrounded her, he was shocked by the power and connection. It scared the hell out of him. He was afraid to be close to that. To touch her, never mind kiss her with his brothers there, too. It was something insane but knowing she was almost taken from them brought on these feeling of protectiveness and possessiveness that he knew only one way to relieve. He needed to hold her. To make sure she was fine, and with him and his brothers where she was safest.

* * * *

"Are you sure that Alessa will be okay with Cobra and them?" Alda asked as she sat in the back of the SUV leaning against Logic's shoulder. She was exhausted, and it was late.

"She's in the safest place she could be. With men that care about her and that will protect her," Royce stated from the driver's seat. Brew was in the passenger seat and hadn't said a word. Logic and Train sat on either side of her and Train's hand caressed her thigh. She had her legs crossed but was leaning into Logic.

She inhaled Logic's cologne and absorbed the feel of having both men so close to her, caressing her, making her feel safe.

"I can't believe Alessa was drugged and that the guy was going to take her home," she said aloud.

"To a party," Train said.

"What?" she asked and lifted up. Train and those dark brown eyes, stern expression and the goatee added to the man's intense demeanor. He and Logic were so big that she was squished between the two of them in the backseat.

"He was going to take her to a party where a group of guys chipped in for the drug," Logic said to her. Tears filled her eyes. Guys did that kind of stuff? Seriously?

"He was going to take you, too, Alda, but you didn't drink the drink that was left for you. Alessa drank hers," Brew stated from the front seat and he sounded so pissed off.

"Through the surveillance video in the club we saw that dick put a pill in each glass. It was while that big guy came over to harass you, wanting to dance," Royce said to her.

"A setup?" she asked, as a tear fell.

"Not sure. Couldn't find that big asshole anywhere," Train told her, then reached over and wiped away the tear from her cheek.

"I can't believe they were going to take Alessa to some party and that guys paid to drug a woman. That's sick," she said, her voice cracking.

"They paid a thousand dollars to bring two women, you and Alessa to a party with a bunch of fucking asshole guys who would do whatever they wanted to you," Brew said. His voice sounding distorted.

"Oh God." She covered her mouth.

Train cupped her cheek and looked into her eyes. "It didn't happen. You're both safe so don't even think about it. You're safe with us, remember that," he told her firmly. She held his gaze and lowered her hand from her mouth.

"It was that easy. It would have been that easy to just take two women of their choosing," she said and gulped.

"Don't," Logic said and squeezed her thigh. She closed her eyes and thought about the situation, and about how she wanted to keep away from these men, when they were the ones looking out to protect her.

She reached out and cupped Train's cheek. "I pushed you all away. What if you weren't watching me? What if —"

Train turned his head and kissed her palm. The SUV stopped and the engine died.

Train looked at her.

"We've always kept eyes on you, Alda. How could we not?" he whispered.

Logic opened the door and offered her a hand. They were walking her up. Maybe staying with her. She didn't know what to do. She didn't want them to leave her, yet she feared knowing that nothing would really come of this thing between them. It would be sex. Just lust, a need deep in their bodies after experiencing this crazy night and thoughts of what could have happened but didn't. She was safe because of them.

She used her card key and punched in the code giving them all access to her apartment building. The anticipation of what would come was overwhelming as they reached the elevator and she debated about making them go home and leaving her here alone. Alone. The thought of it made her shake. She kept a hand over her waist where the tear was and the bandage that was below it. Train hit the floor number and the doors closed. They were quiet.

Brew remained facing away from her as he rubbed his jaw. Train placed his hands on her shoulders then rubbed her arms and pulled her into an embrace, her back against his front. She leaned back, absorbing the masculinity and the scent of his cologne. The doors opened and they headed out and down the hallway to her door. It was surreal. Having all four men here with her in the small hallway about to enter her apartment and more than likely make love to her. She reached into her small purse for the keys and her hand was shaking. Train covered it with his. "Relax," he told her as she looked up into his eyes.

He opened the door and they all walked inside. She noticed that Logic looked around the place, but Brew stood there breathing funny, rubbing his jaw and looking intense.

"Great place. It's pretty big," Logic told her.

"Thank you. It's more than enough room for me."

"What made you choose this neighborhood?" Train asked her.

"The security, and the school right next door."

"Plus this view of the park, too, huh?" Royce asked, looking out the side window.

She looked back at Brew. He appeared extremely serious as his eyes landed on her.

"Brew, what's—"

"Don't," he snapped at her and she gasped. Felt her heart racing.

"Brew," Royce said his name and his tone warning, and then suddenly the man stomped toward her. Brew pulled her into his arms and hugged her tight. He held her so snuggly and with such intensity to what she felt that she hugged him back as tears fell from her eyes and she kissed his neck.

She could hear his rapid breathing, feel his palms smooth all over her back, then her ass as he turned his face, she sought out his mouth as he lowered down and kissed her. It was wild, and she never in her entire life felt so turned on and out of control. She wanted his hands everywhere. Their hands and mouths everywhere. When he unzipped her dress and started backing her up, she pulled back and started to unbutton his shirt. Her dress began to fall and he pushed her hands away from his shirt, lifted her up and against him as she straddled his waist and he carried her down the hallway.

She wanted, needed this so badly and kissed him on the mouth hard. He pressed her up against the wall right before the bedroom and thrust his hips against her mound. She kissed him deeper, ran her fingers through his hair and cupped his cheeks. When she pulled from his lips he looked insane.

"Tell me you're on the pill, baby. I want nothing between us."

She stared down into his eyes as he pulled back and started bringing her into the bedroom.

"I have an IUD but you should use something." He lowered her feet to the floor in front of the bed. The others joined them, undressing, looking hungry and needy.

"No. We're safe," he told her. His hard, commanding voice shocked her system and he started kissing her neck and reaching behind her to undo her bra.

"Seriously, Brew, you have a reputation," she told him.

He lifted up and cupped her cheeks, staring down into her eyes.

"I've never had sex without a condom. This is fucking different. I want. I need all of you with no barriers, Alda. Now I didn't ask for any proof that you are on birth control, did I?" he asked her and she got it. He wasn't playing games and neither was she. This was special. There were no lies, no more walls, everything came down tonight.

She nodded her head and he let her bra fall from her breasts.

"Fuck," Royce whispered, climbing up onto the bed behind her and leaning closer to kiss her skin. She felt the hands on her hips and then fingers explore her tattoo of cherry blossoms along her hip and to her belly.

She glanced at Logic as he entwined their hands, brought hers to his lips and kissed the top before he licked his lips, eying over her breasts as his other fingers caressed the bandage on her hip. Logic looked so serious and emotional. Like he was truly upset that she had a bandage, a cut on her hip and had been hurt.

Brew undressed quickly and Train took her other hand, brought her fingers to his lips and kissed them. She was surrounded by four extremely sexy, muscular men and they all wanted her.

"Oh God," she whispered as Brew lowered down in front of her, kissing along her belly and the belly ring. The tattoos and muscles were everywhere. His expression so hard, demanding, wild, it both scared her and turned her on. His fingers started to push her panties down, then he pressed his nose to her mound and inhaled against the material. Was that a growl? She shivered.

Simultaneously, Train and Logic leaned down and suckled her breasts. She felt each tongue lap at her nipples and then suckle nipple and some breast into their mouths as if starving to enjoy her flesh. Then came the lick along her ass cheeks and then her crack. Royce. Holy God, four men were feasting on her. With them restraining her she felt her pussy spasm and she closed her eyes and moaned.

Royce took her hands from Train and Logic and pulled them behind her back and over his cock. She gasped, and wondered how the hell she was even standing up.

"Feel what you do to me, baby. How hard you make my cock. Watching this sexy ass in all those damn tight ass dresses you wear to the clubs. I've wanted to see you naked for so fucking long, never mind wanted to sink my cock deep into your cunt," Royce said, kissing along her neck and rocking his cock between her fingers.

"Oh Royce. Really?" she asked him, sounding breathless.

"Really," he said and suckled her neck on her shoulder.

"We all have," Logic stated, releasing her breast and licking along the tip again and sucking hard.

Brew took that moment to slide fingers into her cunt.

"So wet for us. My God, Alda, your pussy is sopping wet," Brew said to her.

Her lips were parted, her breathing rapid and she felt the orgasm building and building.

"I need a taste," Brew said, thrusting his fingers up into her cunt, making her moan louder. He lowered to the floor, lifted her thigh over his shoulder and latched on to her clit. She fell slightly back against Royce, unable to remain balanced as she was still restrained and being feasted on. It was so wild. Brew suckled hard as she took in the sight of all their muscles, the tattoos and the way they worked together to arouse her and make her come. She was close. So damn close.

Slowly Royce moved out of the way, releasing her hands. Her back hit the comforter and all four men attacked. Brew was sucking and stroking her pussy, his head between her thighs that were over his shoulders. He was filled with muscles, and loaded with black tattoos everywhere she could see. Intricate ones, wild ones, some scary, some just patterns and designs. Her hands were pushed up over her head, causing her breasts to lift up, her hips to raise, and Royce was there lowering down to kiss her mouth. Train and Logic continued to feast on her breasts, following her movement as they manipulated her body to their liking. Tongues and fingers trailed along her skin, then on her ribs and the tattoo she had.

"You are gorgeous, baby. I never would have imagined you with a tattoo," Logic said and trailed a finger along the tattoo.

Royce released her lips and Brew lifted his mouth off her cunt. "Delicious," he hissed. Brew looked at her with determination and desire in his eyes, licking his lips and then lifting a very thick big cock with his hand.

"Mine," he said and then climbed up higher, spread her thighs wider as the others moved but Royce kept her restrained and Brew began to push his cock into her pussy.

"Let me in. Come on now, baby. Let me in."

He hovered above her, slid his palms over her breasts, cupped them and lowered down to lick the tips. He was torturing her, nudging his cock deeper and deeper.

"Brew, please. Please," she begged, widened her thighs and tilted her pelvis up. He slid his palms up her arms. Royce released his hold on her and Brew took complete control. She was shocked at his strength, his size and very intimidated by the plethora of tattoos and muscles. He pulled back and thrust into her fully. Her lips parted. She felt her pussy stretch to accommodate his thick, long cock. Alda lifted her chin and cried out as he began to thrust in and out of her cunt slowly but with purpose.

"Look at me. Fucking look at me while I make love to you, baby! I told you this was different. Never like this, Alda. Never," he stated and began to thrust harder, faster, gripping her shoulders and pounding into her body. She loved it. She felt a mix of uncertainty and need and it caused her body to erupt as she cried out her release.

"So hot and sexy. Look at her. Look at our woman," Train said and reached over and pinched her nipple.

"Oh," she said and Brew thrust faster and harder into her.

"Never like this, Alda. Never. God damn, her pussy is gripping my cock. Fuck. There. So fucking there," he said. He gripped her shoulders and thrust so hard and deep she lost her breath and he roared as he came inside of her.

Brew ran his palms up her arms to her hands and entwined them. She stared up into his dark brown eyes as he lowered down and kissed her, using those thick, hard muscular arms to remain above her, to not crush her. He was massive.

His lips parted like he was going to say something more and then he lowered down and kissed her lips, released her hands and then released her.

Their lips parted and she caressed his chest with her palm as he sat up above her. He gripped her wrist. She squinted at him, feeling shocked and like maybe he didn't like being touched or something. But what they just shared was incredible.

He looked away and at Royce. "She packs one hell of a punch, bro," Brew said and eased out of her and stood up. Royce stood in front of her at the edge of the bed. She started to close her legs and he shook his head.

"You ready for me, baby?" he asked and holy God, her pussy throbbed and erupted. Royce stood before her completely naked, standing over six feet three inches tall, tan, muscular with dark brown hair, wide eyes that made her feel like he had the capabilities to see into her soul, and such a dominant expression on his face. He always seemed like the one in charge, and was always giving orders.

He raised one of his eyebrows at her non-verbal response while he reached out and stroked her breast.

"Yes," she said, sounding breathless to her own ears. He licked his lips and eased a thigh between her legs.

His fingers trailed along her tattoo and to her pussy and thigh. She wiggled and began to close her legs but his thick hard thigh was there.

"Don't move," he whispered.

She stared at him in adoration and need.

"Arms above your head. Thighs open for me," he told her and her heart felt like it was going to explode from her chest.

She had been scared, angry, jealous about their experiences with other women, but right now as they used their tools, their obvious knowledge of a woman's body on her she didn't mind one bit at all. He hadn't even fucked her yet and she was moving, lifting her hips, practically moaning.

He looked at her eyes, her lips, her breasts, and her pussy.

"Exceptional. Absolutely exceptional," he complimented then eased over her, cupped her face between his hands and forearms and kissed her tenderly. She felt the thick, hard, weight of his body crush against her. Instinctively she lifted her thighs up against his hips and his thick cock and full balls pressed against her pussy lips. His hands eased up her arms as he pulled from her lips and lifted up, holding her gaze.

"Remind me again, why we've been fighting this attraction, brothers," he said to the others. She found it endearing that he called them his brothers, not his friends. It exemplified the closeness and connection they shared. She felt as if she was part of it, even if just for tonight.

He eased the tip of his cock to her pussy as he released her arms and cupped her breast. He used his other hand to grip his cock.

"Open, and let me in. I'm claiming this pussy, this body completely tonight. Understood?" he asked. She nodded but her heart, her gut clenched with a slight confusion as to what he meant. Was this a one night thing? A way to satisfy this lustful desire tonight or was it more? Was it deeper? Did she want it to be deeper? Did she expect—

She gasped as he thrust into her fully in one hard stroke. She lifted her arms to his shoulders.

"No. Arms up. I'll let you touch me in a minute. I need to feel control right now, Alda. I need control," he stated through clenched teeth. She lifted her arms back, tilted her hips up and widened her thighs as he thrust into her faster, deeper. He gripped her hips and pulled her thighs up over his hips and pounded into her. Her ass and lower half lifted off the bed and he thrust and thrust, taking her breath away.

"Never letting you out of my sight. Never. Understand me?" Royce roared and stroked and she cried out, coming and shaking at his control, his thrusts and possessiveness of her body.

"Fuck. I can't last. Holy fuck, I can't," he said and then lowered down and thrust and stroked into her until he grunted and came. He immediately kissed her mouth and rolled to his side to caress her ass and let her hug him. She ran her fingers through his hair and their lips touched numerous times, kissing, pecking, exploring. She nuzzled into his shoulder and he squeezed her so tight to him she thought he might crush her ribs. "Oh," she exclaimed and he mumbled.

Smack.

She gasped, shocked that he smacked her ass.

"You are a feminine, sweet beauty who needs big time protection." He gripped her chin and jaw.

"No other men. Ever," he commanded. She stared at his eyes and his lips but didn't answer. He squinted and then eased out of her, as Logic slid in behind her and began to caress her thigh and then her ass. He moved her to her belly and she moaned as he began to massage her.

* * * *

Logic's heart was racing, his cock throbbing and a thousand thoughts ran through his mind. The four of them never took a woman together. Never really wanted to, yet here they were with Alda, one exceptionally sexy, classy, gorgeous woman and the thoughts were all over the place. Possessiveness, control, domination, desire, jealousy, it was never ending, his mind erupting in fears he never had. This was insane, intense and all he wanted to do was possess her. Their goddess. The woman they fought so hard to resist and stay clear of. He thought hearing about her with the other guy last night was bad and pissed him off, but tonight's incident scared the crap out of him and his brothers. Brew was a nightmare, ready to kill and leave a bloody massacre in his path, the others felt the same way. Logic, however, was relieved that Alda and her friend were safe. What he hadn't expected was the intensity, the deep need he had to claim her and with his brothers, no less. Watching them dominate her, make love to her, and mark her their woman together was territory they knew nothing about.

"That feels good, Logic." She moaned as he straddled her legs and ass and massaged her shoulders, her sexy back and then over her hip, the surprisingly sexy tattoo and her perfect ass.

"You feel good, Alda. Your skin is flawless, your body perfection," he said to her.

He lowered down and started to kiss her neck, her shoulders and down her spine. His thick cock hardened the lower he got and then he licked and nipped her ass, making her gasp and shake.

"Such a perfect ass. I've watched this sexy ass in some pretty revealing dresses, Alda. Thought about how if you were my woman only my brothers and I would get to touch this ass, caress it while we fucked it and spanked it."

"Logic," she moaned. He massaged her ass cheeks and then spread her thighs. Logic slid a finger into her pussy and she lifted her hips.

"We're going to claim every inch of you, Alda. It's going to take fucking you in every hole to get rid of this fear, this need for control to dissipate." He slid a slick finger up over her anus and began to press in when she gasped and tried turning. He gripped her hips.

"Whoa, sweetie, what's wrong?" he asked and leaned to the side to look into her eyes.

"Tell me. Don't you like what I'm doing?"

"Yes."

"Then why did you pull away?"

Train climbed onto the bed. He reached over and caressed her hair.

"We're going to want all of you. Don't hold back," Train said to her.

She pulled her lower lip between her teeth and Logic lifted her hips up. "On all fours. I need in," he said to her and she tightened up.

"Not my ass though," she said and he squinted at her. He caressed her ass and then eased a finger into her pussy.

She moaned.

"Why not, baby? We'll go slow. Take you nice and easy," he said to her.

"I never did that before. I've never been with more than one man at a time, Logic," she said and his heart pounded faster.

"A virgin ass? Oh, man," Train said and eased his palm along her ass then smacked it.

Her expression changed and she looked embarrassed, maybe shy at the fact.

Logic wrapped an arm around her waist and leaned over her with his fingers slowly stroking her cunt.

"I think that's super sexy, Alda. That you never let a man fuck your ass. We'll be your firsts, when you're ready for that." He kissed her neck and then stroked a little faster. She seemed to relax and his mind began to process his feelings and his thoughts. This sure was different. She was special in so many ways. He kind of felt like a dick, yet then his thoughts became so possessive he wanted to keep her his woman forever. It was shocking.

He started to rock his hips and she lowered down and lifted her ass upward. She was ready for him. He couldn't take waiting any longer. All these months watching her, desiring her, yearning to see what she looked like naked, and sounded like while she came.

He eased his fingers out and replaced them with his cock. He slowly pressed into her just as Train cupped her cheek and brought his cock to her lips.

"I need to, baby. It's torture going last. Next time I go first," he said and winked at her. She opened for him slowly, hesitantly like she wasn't used to giving head. Even that aroused Logic. He gripped her hips and began to increase his speed as he watched Alda take more of Train's cock into her mouth. Train closed his eyes and exhaled.

"Mercy, the woman is a natural," he said and gripped her hair. She tightened up and Logic lost it. She was so sensual, inexperienced and it did something to him. He rocked and thrust then grunted as he came. Train pulled his cock from her mouth and she gasped and then moaned, shaking and coming, too.

"My turn. Now," Train demanded. Logic slid from her pussy, let his palms massage and squeeze her ass as Train lifted her onto his chest and kissed her tenderly. Alda straddled Train's waist and kissed him back, ran her palms up his chest until Train gripped them behind her back and hoisted her up so he could suckle her breasts. Her head fell back and she moaned and gasped. "Train! Oh my God. Oh," she exclaimed.

* * * *

Train couldn't seem to get enough of her. He wanted to mark her his woman, too. Claim her with his brothers, the only men he trusted. No woman was ever shared like this between them. Sure, maybe two at a time but that was about it. They never were compelled to all share the same woman, never mind all be attracted like this to only one. She was so sexy, beautiful, and had a killer body. He suckled her tit harder and tugged and nipped at it. She wiggled in his arms and he realized how feminine and weak she was in comparison to him, to any man wanting to possess this body. If that guy had been successful in drugging her she would have been raped by a bunch of men, treated like some animal, some plaything instead of the precious, beautiful woman she was. Fuck. He rolled her to her back and aligned his cock with her cunt. Her hands were stuck underneath her and he cupped her cheek with one hand and gripped his cock with the other. "You are always safe with us. Always, Alda. Remember that." Her eyes widened and she was wiggling to get her arms free when he thrust into her deeply and her large breasts lifted and swayed. The more he thrust and the faster he stroked they would bounce and he couldn't take it. He lifted her up to kiss her mouth and her arms freed and then reached for him. He lowered her back down and she reached up and gripped his shoulder. He gripped her shoulder and he pounded into her, locked gazes with her gorgeous green eyes and it was like everything cleared. All the crazy thoughts, the fears, the lack of desire and need to commit and trust came crashing down and suddenly he saw Alda. She was special. So fucking special that immediately his heart, that was cold, broken, fearless, reacted. It pissed him off and he realized he wasn't ready. He couldn't be ready. Where the fuck did she come from?

He gripped her hips and then felt his orgasm moving closer.

He lifted up, pulled out of her cunt and then flipped her to her belly. She screeched but held on to the comforter as he lifted her hips and aligned his cock with her pussy, stroking right into her from behind.

He eased his hands along her ass and looked at his brothers. They watched in awe. Their raw expressions were how he felt. Shocked, hungry, possessive. It was like they were ready to fuck her all over again. It was going to be a long night. A long fucking night indeed. He thrust and thrust, then slapped her ass and she cried out and came. He eased his fingers under her to her cunt and then brought that cream to her anus and pressed right into her ass.

"Train!" She screamed out and he thrust both cock and finger into her as she panted and panted for breath. Brew was back on the bed, gripped her hair and brought her mouth to his cock. She ate at it hungrily, obviously feeling the desire, the lust he felt. Train was fighting his thoughts, his needs and the truth of what was happening here. He stared at the tattoo along her hip, at the swell of her ass as he fingered her while fucking her pussy. It was different. He wanted her to belong to him and his brothers only. No other men ever again. No other man was allowed to kiss her, hold her, dance with her, run a hand over her ass as he hugged her.

"Fuck! Fuck! Fuck." He thrust so hard so fast he came inside of her.

As she slowed down and felt dizzy, he eased out of her and Royce was there to take his place. Logic grabbed on to Train's shoulder.

"I know, man. I know," was all he said and then looked as shocked as Train felt.

Brew grunted and then came in her mouth. Royce was thrusting into her pussy and fingering her ass, too.

"It's going to be a long night, bro, but in the end, I think we're still going to feel the same things. I want her. Always," Logic said to him and then slid onto the bed and watched his brothers make love to her one more time.

Chapter 6

Lenox, Cobra, Roman, and Ziek watched over Alessa all night. She woke up several times acting like she was completely intoxicated, and even started to undress then kiss Cobra. He was still trying to get over that, and her expressed desires that she wanted them in her bed and to claim her their woman already. They didn't know if it was the truth or not, but boy, did hearing her say the words and basically attack them and kiss them, confuse the hell out of them. They had to hold her down and talk calmly to her to get her to relax and fall back to sleep.

He and the guys talked about how bad this drug was, and how pissed off they were knowing some piece of shit could very well have gotten her out of the club if it weren't for Alda. Their buddies Brew, Royce, Logic, and Train were fuming mad and so damn pissed when the guy said he put something in Alda's drink too but she didn't drink it, that Brew nearly killed the guy on the spot. Staring at Alessa as she slept in her bed had him feeling the same jealous, angry feelings for the guy responsible. He wanted to find the source, the supplier of this very unique and expensive drug.

"Hey, Andreas is on the phone. He got a hold of a number for that guy at the club. It's no longer in service," Lenox said to him.

"They're on to us. They must have heard about last night and the two women being connected to the families. It has to be," Cobra replied.

"Word travels fast when Brew is pissed off and wants heads on platters. Man, I thought he was going to kill that guy."

"I thought of doing it myself," Cobra said and then looked back to the bed where Alessa lay sleeping. She was still wearing the sexy dress, but her feet were bare, the feminine red toenails peeking out from under the covers.

"Cobra, Roman, and Ziek want these guys, just as badly as the rest of us do. We need to get someone over here to keep watch over Alessa while we go hunting. Bella and Caprice will be here in an hour or so," Lenox told him.

"Good, and some guards, too, right?"

"Definitely," Lenox said and then Cobra watched Lenox walk closer to the bed and caress her hair.

"She's too sweet, too angelic to have come so close to such monsters. If they got her to that party…fuck," Lenox said, pulling back and running his fingers through his hair.

The floor creaked and Cobra saw Ziek and Roman.

"Did she awake again?" Ziek asked just as Alessa started to blink open her eyes. Lenox was closest and bent down by the side of the bed. Her eyes landed on him.

"Easy, baby. How are you feeling?" he asked her and she blinked several times and then looked at him wide eyed and then toward the others. She blinked again as if she thought she was imagining seeing them there. She wouldn't know how she came on to them, and how they had to stop her from undressing and rocking her body against theirs one by one, every chance she got.

"My head hurts. I don't feel good. I think I drank too much," she said and Ziek brought over the pail they had by her last night when she said she was going to vomit but didn't.

She tried lifting up. Lenox spoke to her. "Easy, honey. It was a hell of a night and moving around too much could make you feel worse," he told her. She looked at him and then the others.

"What happened? What are you doing here?" she asked and tears instantly filled her eyes, and she pulled the blankets on the bed higher against her body.

"You don't remember what happened last night?" Ziek asked her, moving closer to the bed. Cobra's stomach ached.

She closed her eyes and then sat up with Lenox's assistance. Her hair was messy and fell over her shoulder. The blankets fell and he could see how loose her dress was. She unzipped it last night and they wouldn't dare re-zip it, afraid that she would kiss them again and undress the rest of the way.

Her large breasts poured from the top and she held it.

"My dress," she said and then looked at them.

"Nothing happened between us and you, honey. We watched over you. Do you remember anything from last night?" Roman asked, sounding so commanding and authoritative. The tears spilled from her eyes as she squinted and then her lip quivered. Lenox reached out and caressed her hair.

"It's okay. Alda and the rest of us saved you."

"Saved me from what?" she asked.

Cobra got angrier. She didn't remember one goddamn thing. No wonder this stuff was so expensive. Anyone who took it had no recollection of the night's events. These women could be raped, tortured by multiple men and she wouldn't even know it unless they left bruises, or did worse things.

Lenox placed his hands over hers as she sat on the side of the bed. Ziek sat next to her and caressed her hair as he helped zip up her dress on the side.

Roman stood by Cobra.

"Someone drugged you last night. They put it in your drink and planned on making you leave with them," Roman explained.

"Drugged me? I was drugged? How did you stop them? Where is Alda? Is she hurt?" she asked.

"Alda is with her men. She saw the guy trying to make you leave and noticed you were acting drunk. The guy tried forcing you out but Alda made a scene." Roman explained in detail what happened and then what they did and what was going on as an inside investigation.

The tears fell and she sniffled and then covered her mouth. "They were going to rape me? Multiple men? Oh my God."

"It's okay, baby. We got to you. We've stayed with you all night," Lenox told her and hugged her to him. She hugged him tight and cried against his chest. Ziek caressed her back and reassured her that she was going to be okay and not to focus on what could have happened and focus on the fact that she was safe and they were all protecting her.

Cobra looked at Roman.

"Bella and Caprice should be here soon and I think we need to start knocking on doors." Roman nodded and then Cobra looked back at Lenox and Ziek consoling sweet, young, beautiful Alessa. A woman ten years younger than them and one they'd had their eyes on but didn't make a move. She was going to get their protection whether she wanted it or not from here on out. He never wanted to feel so helpless and worried again.

* * * *

It cost Antonio a lot of fucking money to clean up the mess of blood. Tatum truly lost his shit and took some seriously nasty crap last night. He caused Antonio to lose the opportunity to get Alda into bed. She seemed ripe for the taking, especially at the bar as she let him run his hands along her skin and practically her ass. He hoped one of those two dicks she was friends with didn't take her home with them. He was making progress. Letting her know that she could be the face for international sales of MAX products. He needed another meeting with her. Preferably, alone.

"I'm sorry I fucked up," Tatum stated from the doorway, holding his head. His eyes were red, his hair a mess. He looked like shit.

"This shit can't happen, Tatum. You promised, never again back in the UK and look what happened?"

"I know. I fucking know, okay. It was the shit I took."

"Where did you get it? Who gave it to you?"

"Haley."

Antonio clenched his teeth. That fucking bitch. She was jealous. Haley knew what he was planning. To seduce Alda, get her into bed and to be the face of MAX products overseas. He'd whisk her away, totally take over her life in every way, and Haley was jealous.

"She shouldn't have given you anything. You don't need it. The point of using that drug on the women is to remain in complete control and get what you want. No harm comes to the women and that's what keeps you out of fucking jail. They don't remember shit, and you get to get off every way you want with their bodies. No bruises, no marks on them. It's foolproof if you just fucking stay off the drugs yourself."

"I know, Antonio. I fucking know but Haley, she came here, wearing one of those sexy dresses, and we drank. She brought a friend."

"A friend you fucked up so bad she might die."

"You'll make sure she doesn't die."

"You think I have control over life and death? Did you not see the fucking blood? The damage you did on that woman?" Antonio yelled. He had to make sure that Tatum didn't know he killed the woman. Tatum would spiral out of control and he would lose his mind completely.

"She'll make it. Tell me she'll make it, Antonio. I need to know that she'll make it."

He stared at him. The man was just as big, as muscular as Antonio was. He was a smart man, a good businessman and this mistake could have cost them everything.

"I just wanted to keep her."

"What?" Antonio asked him.

"I know. I know it's fucked up, but I'm tired of no connections, of these games we've played perfecting the drug. It's perfect now. We know that and are making a killing in sales. I want a woman that will stay with me."

Antonio exhaled. He didn't want to mention what he was working on.

"Haley said there's a woman that would be perfect for me." Antonio's chest tightened. Haley must have mentioned Alda to him. Shit, she wasn't ready yet. Antonio needed time.

"Haley showed me a picture of her, Antonio. She's perfect. Definitely not like the others. It's time to stop fucking around."

"And if you took something out of boredom again and hurt Alda?"

"I won't. It was Haley's doing. She slipped it into my drink. I should have known something was up when she kissed me and her friend she brought got this dazed look in her eyes and I knew. Haley brought her for me, but wanted to join in, too. It was too late when I started feeling funny and then things got out of hand."

"Yes, they did get out of hand and Haley will suffer for it, as well."

Antonio had his hands on his hips as he looked out at the city skyscrapers.

"Can I meet her?" Tatum asked.

"Not yet. She isn't ready yet, and I'm not sure she's right for this or even available."

"What do you mean? Haley said she doesn't date and works a lot."

"When I was out with her there were men around that knew her. Made men she was friends with. There could be something there."

"No. No, you'll make sure we get her. I want it to be her. She looks like a model, and Haley said she's smart, classy and knows the product line. Between the two of us, you and I, we can make her ours. We can use her as the face for the products and smuggle the drugs in and out of the country in those makeup packages. It's going to work."

"I don't know, Tatum."

Tatum was quiet.

"You want her for yourself. She's that perfect, isn't she? Holy fuck, Antonio."

Antonio turned to look at Tatum.

"She's special, Tatum. When you do get to meet her, when I say it's time, you'll realize how special she is and you'll understand that we can't fuck it up. You can't take any drugs, or hurt her. You can't. She's a grand prize in all of this shit we've been doing. Perfecting the drug, marketing it as a very unique and powerful gift. The demand is so high right now that the orders are coming in and we don't have enough product. The best thing I did was put a hold on it for some time."

"When can I see her, meet her?" Tatum asked.

He looked Tatum over.

"When you're out of your funk. When your head is out of your ass and you're cleaned up and sharp minded. Don't trust Haley, no matter what she offers you, understand me?"

"I get it now. The bitch could only get away with fooling me once. She got me when I was down, and wanting more."

"I understand. I'll take care of the other situation, but you need to be sure about remaining calm and not losing your shit. Alda will see right through you."

"She sounds amazing."

Antonio smirked. "Tatum, she is incredible. She's gorgeous, sexy as sin, but there's this air of classiness, confidence, sexuality that would make any man do whatever it takes to keep her close. Her scent, the shampoo, her perfume, whatever it is makes you want to lean closer and inhale. She's feminine, too, and submissive."

"Fuck," Tatum said and swallowed hard. "How much longer, Antonio?"

"Friday night they'll be a party. A pre-release celebration for one of the other lines MAX Industries is launching. She'll be there. Working it, of course, but I won't introduce you. You'll need to make your own introductions and see if the attraction is there. If it goes well then we'll set up another meeting with her alone."

"Good. Very good. I'll be fine by Friday. I'll get it together and won't fuck up again. What about Haley?"

"Oh, don't worry about her. I'll take care of Haley personally. The bitch has obviously forgotten who owns her."

* * * *

Alda awoke with her face wedged up between thick, hard muscle. There was a hand pressed over her ass and another one cupped her breast. She instantly felt panicked. Her mind thinking, processing what happened last night. How many times she had sex with Brew, Royce, Logic, and Train. God, it was amazing and she nearly had anal sex, too. What the hell was she thinking? She absorbed the feel of Logic's hand on her breast, his thick body pressed up behind her and her face against Train's chest. Train's hand remained over her ass and now that she was awake, even with her eyes closed he must have been awake too as his hand began to caress along her thigh.

The awkward morning after. How would they react? Where were Brew and Royce? Would they minimize what occurred last night? Was she just another notch on their belts? God, she hoped not, yet she wondered how this could work. It really couldn't work. Not with their professions and certainly not now with hers.

She opened her eyes and began to lift up when the two hands squeezed her, Logic's against her breast and Train's over her ass and thigh. Apparently it didn't bother Train that his brother's hand was over her breasts and against Train's skin. They were close. She remembered them referring to one another as bros throughout the night.

"Good morning," Train said and eased back slightly to look at her. She blinked her eyes, feeling tired still.

The hand that held her ass now eased up her hip to her shoulder then her cheek. She lifted higher.

"Tired still?" he asked.

"A little," she whispered.

Logic stroked her nipple. Her lips parted.

"You were incredible last night, Alda," he said to her and gazed over her lips and her breast, watching Logic stroke her nipple then tug.

"Logic," she whispered. He slid his hand away and to her hip then kissed her neck.

"It's getting late. We should get up, eat something," Logic said and lifted up.

She realized they were starting to make their departure. Brew and Royce already left, their words to her last night were lies told in the heat of passion. Why did it hurt so much knowing they left, that it meant nothing to them? She knew she took a chance last night. There was no way she wasn't going to explore her feelings and give in to the desires.

"You're right. We need to get up. I want to call and check on Alessa," she said as Logic climbed out of her bed. Train squinted at her and then caressed her hip.

"We'll check with Cobra and see if Alessa is up yet. Those drugs were strong," he said to her and then stroked her jaw, just staring at her like Train wanted to say more, or perhaps was still thinking about the possibility that it could have been her drugged last night, too. Could he care so much, or was it all part of the game, the role he was playing right now?

"Okay. I should shower first."

He nodded and then got up, offered her a hand and when she moved she felt achy, sore in places she wasn't used to feeling sore in.

"Are you okay?" he asked her with a hand on her hip, once again his eyes zeroed in on her body, making every inch react with need and desire. She loved the way he looked at her like she was a feast.

Perfection and more than he expected. Was it foolish for her to wish last night meant more to him and the others?

"Maybe a bath instead?" he suggested, holding her by her hips.

"I'll be fine. Help yourselves to whatever you want in the kitchen," she told him and he nodded and then released her but one glance over her shoulder and both men were staring at her body.

She closed the bathroom door and leaned against it, exhaling.

"Oh God, I like them so much. How could I be so stupid? How could I let them into my body and my heart? I was just going to be another woman who had sex with them and now lusted over them." Her heart ached and she felt stupid, used, and she didn't like the feeling. She needed to be smart here. It was a great night, brought on by a dangerous and terrible situation. No woman would have been able to resist their masculinity, their commands and instant protectiveness. The four men acted possessive, protective and like she was their top priority. So what it was just as precaution and an after effect of the situation. It was still enjoyable. Hell, it was incredible, who was she kidding. She pushed off the door and turned on the shower, grabbing what she needed. She looked in the mirror and could see the glow on her face, the love bites along her skin, her breasts. She pressed fingers to them and traced the light marks. Four men. Brew, Royce, Logic, and Train, enforcers, soldiers, made men and she had sex, a ménage for the very first time with the four of them. Holy shit.

She got into the shower and gave herself a mental pep talk. It was time to face the realities of what she engaged in last night. If the four men could act so nonchalant and unaffected by it, then she could do that, too. She was a professional woman who faced aggressive businessmen in meeting rooms, certainly she could handle a one-night stand with four sexy, oh God, amazing lovers like these guys. "Shit," she stated aloud and felt too many emotions to process. She finished up and dried herself off. She then did her hair and makeup, very little makeup. She wasn't too into it at all. She dressed casually. An off the shoulder long sleeve top that hugged her shape and a pair of hip hugger designer jeans that showed off her belly ring, and a bit of the tattoo on her hip. If she was going to be released like their latest adventure then she might as well make them drool as they left her this morning.

* * * *

They had taken quick showers in the guest bathroom down the hallway and now waited in the kitchen. Logic looked at Train.

"They fucking left, what did they say in the text?" Logic asked.

"That Andreas picked up on a guy who knows more information about the drugs. They needed backup."

"Shit, I hope they can track whomever the supplier is. What did Cobra say about Alessa?" Logic asked.

"She's very upset, but relieved that Alda was keeping eyes on her and that everyone was there to save her. Cobra is so pissed off," Train stated.

"I bet he is. They care for her. Maybe this is a step in letting her know how they feel?"

Train gave him a sideways look. "Seriously? That is not going to happen any time soon. They're too stubborn."

"Kind of like we are," Logic said and then turned to look toward Alda's bedroom.

"What are we going to do about Alda? About last night?"

"I don't know. I mean, I fucking know what I want to do but Brew and Royce think we need to wait. To resolve this situation with the drugs."

"We're all busy right now. I say we take our time with this."

"Take our time? What the fuck, Train. I want her. In our lives. In our beds."

"I don't want to fuck this up and I think considering how fucking powerful it was last night, us sharing her, I think we need to go slow and not rush things."

The sound of her phone going off caught their attention. Logic reached for it off the table. He squinted.

"Antonio?"

"The guy she was with at the bar?"

Logic looked at Train and then set the phone back down.

"We wait. No drastic changes over one night."

"Says the man who doesn't cuddle or stay with a woman in bed all night."

"Like you ever fucking stayed the night with a woman and had conversation in the morning," Train challenged.

"Her body is fucking perfection."

"She's perfection."

"It was more than just sex."

"Of course it was, Logic, but we all need time to process this. Let's handle the situation. Be calm, don't overreact, and leave things on a calm neutral note before we leave and go help Brew, Royce, and the others."

"So, does anyone want coffee?" Alda asked, walking into the room. Holy fuck, Logic felt his heart race, his cock harden and that damn need to possess her come full circle as he took in the sight of her.

One glance at Train and he knew his brother felt it, too.

"Sure," Train said and approached her.

Logic was in a dead stare at the beauty. The hip hugging jeans, her taut belly and belly ring, the skin on her off the shoulder top and those high-heeled boots she wore all turned him on. She was classy, sexy, and so fucking calm. Calmer than he felt. Was she used to this? Not affected by last night like he was?

She went about making the coffee as Train leaned against the counter watching her.

Train reached out and took her hand.

"You feeling okay?" he asked. She smiled.

"I feel fine." Train slid his hand along her hip to her ass and pulled her close. She gripped on to his arms.

"Brew and Royce had to go help Andreas with a few things. They also talked to Cobra and Alessa is doing better. Just really upset."

"I should go see her this morning so we can talk about things."

Train reached up and stroked her cheek.

"Yeah, that would be helpful to her, I'm sure. We have things to get done."

"Okay," she said and pulled back. Logic saw Train's expression.

"Your phone has been going off a lot," Logic said and she turned to look at him.

"Oh, maybe the girls calling to find out about last night. I'm sure everyone heard by now. Alessa's place will be packed. We should organize bringing over some stuff and hanging out for the day with her," she said as she looked at her phone. Logic saw her eyes squint and then she smirked. Was she smirking at something the guy Antonio sent her? She scrolled down.

"Yup, lots of missed text messages." She looked flushed. What did that guy say to her to make her blush?

Logic reached for her hand and pulled her into his arms. She held his gaze as he inhaled her shampoo, and the feel of her gorgeous body in his arms.

"We can drive you to Alessa's place."

"Oh, that's okay." She glanced at her phone. "Bella is coming with Jack and Covan. They're picking me up on their way." He didn't like how distant she sounded and like she was putting up walls. Like last night didn't matter.

"We'll wait for them to get here and make sure you're safe," he said to her and looked at her lips.

"You don't need to, I mean if there's some place else you'd rather, I mean you need to be. Like Brew and Royce," she added.

"We wait," Train said, walking closer. Logic felt angry, possessive. He didn't want to leave her. He didn't want to show how much this woman affected him but she did. He cupped her cheek, ran his hand under her hair and kissed her. He used his other hand to caress her skin where it lifted on her hip then Train joined in. Kissing her neck, gripping her hips and then cupping her breast. She moaned into Logic's mouth and he felt so fucking needy. It was like he needed her again. They were at it all night. Got hardly any sleep, and he was needing more of her.

She started pulling back and when Logic released her lips, Train gripped her hair and tilted her head toward him and Logic released her to him. Train kissed her deeply, dipped her in his arms and then continued to cup her breast and then her ass. She slid her thigh up against his waist and then he released her lips and hugged her.

They didn't say a word to her. Didn't ask when they could see her again. They never did any of this type of thing before. Never slept over at the woman's place or stayed long enough to share a morning after, never mind want more.

"Oh, the coffee. Let's have some before they get here," she said and slid from Train's arms. Logic watched Train rub along his jaw, place a hand on his hip and exhale, watching Alda's sexy ass walk away. He glanced at Logic and Logic couldn't help but feel confused and just like what Train looked like.

"How do you like your coffees? I have creamer, flavored creamers, milk," she said to them.

"Black will be perfect," Train said and walked back into her kitchen. Logic followed. The rest of the day was going to suck. This just didn't feel right at all.

* * * *

"So they left before you even woke up?" Bella asked Alda.

Alda nodded and took a sip from her water bottle. Caprice, Bella, Giada, Alessa, Gisella, and Donata were there at Alessa's apartment. They talked about what happened at the club and then about their nights.

"But Logic and Train kissed you, and they stayed, so Brew and Royce probably didn't have much of a choice," Donata stated.

"No, it was different. They put up the walls. Acted like they felt uncomfortable being there. I suppose they're used to just having sex with women then leaving them," Alda said and felt sick to her stomach. She wondered why it hurt so badly. She knew what she was getting herself into.

"I don't know, I think there's more to it," Bella said to her.

"How can you think that, Bella? You and Giada have been around Brew, Royce, Logic, and Train long enough to see them in action and to know they don't date. They fuck," Donata stated.

"As do a lot of the men, but obviously it was different," Bella stated.

"How so?" Alda asked.

"They were lunatics over what happened. Brew, Royce, Logic, and Train as well as Lenox, Roman, and Ziek were insane last night. I overheard Major and Fedarro talking all the men down before they did something rash. They were all concerned for you, Alda, and for you, Alessa," Bella told them.

"How did things go with you, Alessa? You were so out of it last night. It was scary to see," Donata asked.

"I don't remember anything. I just kind of got the feeling that I may have done or said something to Lenox, Cobra, Roman or Ziek. I don't know. I just couldn't believe that they took care of me and stayed with me all night. Then when they told me the guys' plans for me when they took me, I lost it and started crying," Alessa said and tears filled her eyes.

"I can't believe that there's a drug like this out there. That people will pay five hundred dollars for one pill. It's sick," Bella said.

"Five hundred dollars for one pill? Where did you hear that?" Alda asked.

Bella raised her eyebrows up at her as if saying *what are you, stupid for asking me that.*

"I hope they catch these guys making this stuff. A woman can't even go out anymore and let loose a little," Donata stated in annoyance.

"You'd better be extra careful, Donata, you go out more than all of us," Giada said to her.

"Yeah, don't be surprised if Turbo, Harley, Covan or Jack have a sit down with you about precautions. I got one, and meanwhile Maverick, Antonio, and Corrano if not Angelo, Vito or Morano make my drinks for me. I'm never even alone at a club or by a bar. They were fierce last night," Caprice said to them.

"Just as Brew, Royce, Logic, and Train sounded like they were with Alda last night," Giada stated and winked.

"How was it? Aside from the fact of being a one-time deal?" Donata asked Alda.

"Hey, it may not have been a one-time deal," Bella stated.

"No, I think she's right. I knew what I was getting into. It was so wild though. The need, the desire after everything that happened. They were intense," Alda said and looked down at her hands.

"Who made the first move?" Giada asked. Alda looked up.

"Brew."

"What?" Giada asked, seeming shocked.

"I know. I mean he was pissed off after talking to the guy that tried taking Alessa, and that cut me. He was so quiet and then when I started to ask him if he was okay, he cut me off with a 'Don't' in that tone of his. It scared me, yet aroused me and the next thing I know he's closing the space between us and pulling me into his arms, kissing me. I'm up against the wall, we're grinding our bodies together and shit, I engaged in a ménage with four made men. Killers, heavies in the mob. What the hell was I thinking?" she asked and covered her face with her hands.

"Holy shit, that sounds so hot. More detail. More, please," Donata asked and they started to laugh.

Alda threw a napkin at Donata.

"What? It sounded so hot and they mauled your body, took you to bed. Who the hell cares if it was a one night?" Donata asked.

"A ménage is pretty powerful, Donata. Multiple men taking from your body, exploring every inch," Caprice told her.

"It sure is…was," Alda said and tears filled her eyes. Bella reached over and covered her hand.

"Aw, honey. It wasn't a one-night stand. There's no way it was," she told her.

"Yeah, no way. Not by their reaction to you being in danger, never mind how pissed they were the other night when they saw you on a date," Giada added.

"A date? With who?" Donata asked.

"It wasn't a date. It was a dinner meeting. This guy who is working with my bosses and negotiating the idea of international sales."

"Oh no, don't tell me you could lose your job again," Gisella added.

"No, the owners actually want to go international, just at their own pace. It's just beginning stages," she told them.

"Then why were you meeting with him, and alone?" Caprice asked.

"My bosses wanted me to in order to maintain the idea of moving slow, and perhaps introducing certain products to the market overseas at a slow pace. It kind of went in a different direction though."

"What do you mean?" Gisella asked her.

"Antonio mentioned me being the image to represent this makeup line coming out in a few months."

"What does that mean? Like modeling?" Bella asked her.

"I think it's more a representation of the brand. Like commercials, ads with my image holding the products as representation to the quality and appeal of them. I really don't know much. He was vague and I get the feeling that it was just brainstorming."

"Well, if it was business then why did the guys seem so pissed off?" Donata asked.

"I don't think they were. Besides, I saw them with a couple of women throwing themselves at them. So when Antonio kept me close I didn't push him away."

"Ohh, so you were trying to make them jealous? Interesting," Bella teased.

"It apparently worked. They couldn't take their eyes off you last night at the club," Donata said.

"Which helped when I needed to stop that guy from taking Alessa," Alda said and reached over and held her hand.

"Thank you again, Alda. I can't believe what happened, and worst of all, not remembering any of it," Alessa said.

"Do you think you'll eventually remember?" Caprice asked.

"I don't know. Some guy, Victor, a doctor or something that Dmitri knows, came here. He assured the guys that I would be okay and that the drug just needed to wear off. That's what Cobra, Ziek, Lenox and Roman told me," Alessa said and they all gave her sympathetic smiles.

"Maybe this will get them moving to admit to their feelings for you and yours for them?" Gisella said to Alessa.

"No. Like Alda said earlier, we aren't going to change who these men are, what they do and stand for. It would be meaningless. Just a lustful attraction and sex. I've only been with one man. You guys know that. I think it's going to take some time to get over what happened, or almost happened to me, and how dangerous it is out there for a woman. I think some changes need to be made, and those changes are in me," Alessa said.

Alda held her gaze and nodded.

"Me, too, Alessa. I'm not saying that last night was a mistake. It wasn't. I enjoyed it. It was incredible, and I knew what I was getting into by accepting them in my bed. Nothing will come of this. Life goes on, and work could potentially take me out of New York, heck, out of the country a lot. Who knows? Things have a way of working themselves out," Alda said, and then forced a smile, when really inside she felt like crying. She really wished things were different and last night meant something special, something real like they all told her making love to her. If not, then avoiding them entirely might be the best option to get through this.

Chapter 7

Haley gasped when Antonio grabbed her by the neck and held her up against the wall. She gripped his wrists, her eyes wide, the fear apparent on her face.

"You remember who owns you and who can destroy you, Haley. You have the nerve to talk back to me?" He raised his voice and she shook her head.

"No. No, Antonio. I'm sorry," she said. He released her throat and she started coughing, holding her neck and looking up at him.

He pointed down at her. "You ever give him drugs, fuck with Tatum again and I'll kill you. Do you understand me?" he stated.

"Yes."

"Good, now let's not waste anymore fucking time. I want you to set up another meeting between myself and Alda, and you, so we can get her on board and move things along with her being the image to the makeup line. You'll ensure that Maxwell approves of this so eventually I can take over all products and this company?" he asked.

"Yes, but I don't know if Alda will accept this position as a model, the image for the makeup products."

"Oh, she will not only do it, she will love it, starting with your push, your orders to get things moving. Have her come into the studio today."

"It's Sunday."

"Exactly, and this is crunch time. Do the works on her, and I mean everything, groomed and prepped for Monday."

"What's Monday?"

"A photo shoot with the products. My people will handle it, and you will put her completely in my hands. By Friday evening Tatum will be ready to meet her." Haley's eyes widened, and then she shook her head.

"Seriously? Why her? What does she have that the others hadn't?" she asked, sounding filled with venom.

Antonio eyed Haley over. "So much. Way more than what we thought we wanted. Tatum is going to want exclusivity."

"I hope if we pull this off that I'll be rewarded for the aggravation and of course for telling you about Alda," Haley said with an attitude.

Antonio grabbed her face and squeezed hard.

"You get Alda to accept it all and quickly. Get her to trust me, to accept me, and you'll be shocked at how well you'll be rewarded." He released her face with a shove and then walked back over toward the door.

"Tomorrow morning, a full day of prepping and dinner with the two of us. I want her overwhelmed this week, exhausted and pliant in my hands. Don't fail me, Haley. You know what happens to those that fail me." He walked out of her office and held in his grin. Alda wouldn't know what hit her.

* * * *

"What do you mean, tomorrow morning? What about tonight? Seriously, Haley? This is a lot to—"

Haley cut her off, not giving Alda time to argue. She had no choice, she was going to some upscale salon and getting the works done, and then off to the studio for lighting arrangements and set up then to dinner with Haley and Antonio. By the time she hung up the phone she was shaking and looked at her friends.

"What was that all about?" Bella asked her and she explained.

Donata whistled. "Damn, woman, it sounds like you're going to be a cover model whether you're ready or not."

"Cover model? No, a representative of the makeup products but I don't know about this. I don't model. I don't know if I can do this, or want this."

"It sounds like an amazing opportunity. How much more will you get paid?" Gisella asked her.

"I don't even know," Alda replied and ran her fingers through her hair and stared at them, feeling shocked.

"Maybe that's what the meeting is about. Negotiations," Giada said.

"You think so?" Alda asked.

"Sounds like it, and if not then you should insist on getting paid more. They're going to work you hard, Alda," Alessa said to her.

"Why do I get the feeling this is going to be one hell of a roller coaster and I'm gonna get tossed off midair," she said and they laughed.

"You, the woman who will face any business challenge? No way. You'll be fine and shine in this. Don't let anything stand in your way, Alda. Enjoy this, it sounds like an amazing opportunity," Giada said to her.

"I sure hope so. I guess things do have a way of working themselves out after all."

* * * *

Royce sat in a meeting with Adelina, Sunny and Vinny to discuss any leads with the drugs. It seemed nothing was even circulating underground or on the black market.

"This isn't necessarily a bad thing. It could mean that whomever has created this drug and is distributing it only want to profit themselves. They don't want to mass produce it," Sunny stated.

"Five hundred dollars for one fucking pill and no one has ripped this guy off and come up with something similar, or maybe tried to find out who he is and get in on the action? It doesn't make any sense.

Not that we want in, we want this shit out of here," Fedarro said to them.

"Well, through the guy we met with on Saturday morning with Andreas and the guys, the drop off location is always at a discrete location and no person to person handoff. Money is placed into a mail drop and the drug picked up elsewhere nearby," Royce told them.

"They're being extra careful. It could be a quick money making scam or the guy has limited product and is trying to move the drug quickly," Collin said to them.

"Could be, or it's a means to cause supply and demand. Tease them, and make them want more. The price goes up and it's harder to get but they'll pay for it because of the results," Adelina said.

"If that's the case then it very well could be a quick money making thing. They're obviously not connected to anyone local or we would catch wind of it," Cobra stated.

"This could be a lost cause. We might need to remain focused on all our clubs and having security, the bartenders keep as best of watch as they can. Then look out for our own," Fedarro said to them.

Royce listened to them talk about a few other business things and his mind drifted to Alda. They were caught up trying to get leads on this drug and dealer, and she had been caught up in work all week and some party for work Friday night. Logic told her they wanted to see her. It was Thursday evening and she texted that she was stuck doing something with work. They weren't happy. So when the meeting ended and Royce, Brew, Logic, and Train headed out, they decided to hit Marconie's, a small little bar restaurant a few blocks from Oliva.

"It's after eight. Nothing from her yet?" Brew asked Logic.

Logic shook his head as they walked into the restaurant and bar. It was pretty crowded for a Thursday night.

"I don't fucking believe it," Train said and Royce caught the direction Train was looking in.

"That's Alda, and she's with that guy," Train said to Logic.

"The guy she was with last week?" Royce asked and looked. The guy looked like some sort of rich asshole, and older than them by a few years if he had to guess.

"What the fuck?" Brew raised his voice. Royce grabbed his shoulder.

"Don't do anything stupid," Royce said and in that moment Alda and the guy stood up from the table and he took her hand and headed to the bar and straight toward them. Logic ordered drinks and the bartender was setting them up.

Alda hadn't even looked up. She was talking to the guy and he was smiling and nodding then adding stuff. They sat halfway between them and Royce watched.

"He's touching her," Brew stated through clenched teeth.

"It's crowded," Train said.

"Fuck, it isn't that crowded that his hand needs to remain on her hip. He's even whispering into her fucking ear. Fuck this," Brew said.

Royce reached for him but Brew moved his arm and Royce shook his head.

"Should we stop him?" Logic asked, not moving. Train didn't either and Royce faced the bar.

* * * *

Alda was staring up into Antonio's dark blue eyes. The man was handsome and charismatic. He had been so helpful all week, making her feel comfortable in the studio and giving her advice. Haley disappeared a little while ago and was talking to some guy by the bar and she hoped she joined them soon. This was feeling kind of intimate and she felt a little unsure. She liked Antonio, but he was much older. That made her think of Brew, Logic, Train, and Royce, yet she knew nothing serious or any kind of commitment would happen with them.

Antonio held her gaze and pressed a strand of hair from her cheek.

"You looked incredible today at the photo shoot. Maxwell was impressed, I think," he said to her and then lowered his hand to her hip. She swallowed hard and as she looked away from the deep gaze of his eyes her eyes landed on Brew Brophy heading toward her.

"I thought you were working," Brew interrupted and Antonio stood up straighter. He pulled her closer to him and Brew looked ready to fight.

"This is business, Brew," she said to him.

He eyed where Antonio had his hands on her.

"Doesn't look like business to me."

She was embarrassed. This was not good at all.

"I think you should calm down, buddy," Antonio challenged.

"Calm down?" He raised his voice and stepped closer. Alda put herself between the two men and held her hands on Brew's chest.

"Brew, don't do this. Please, you're embarrassing me," she said to him.

He squinted at her.

"What's going on here, Alda?" Haley approached.

"Brew, please," she pleaded with him and he pulled her a few steps away and wrapped his arms around her. He placed his hand over her ass, making it pretty obvious that he felt he owned her.

"You blow us off for this rich prick."

"Brew, stop it."

"Everything okay over here?" She looked up to see Royce, Logic, and Train.

She pushed from Brew's arms and saw the angry expressions on Antonio and Haley's faces. These guys totally embarrassed her.

"Everything is fine," she said to Royce and then looked at Antonio and Haley.

"These are friends of mine," she introduced them but the men didn't shake hands.

It was awkward and then Haley spoke.

"Alda, walk us out, please," she said to her and Alda gave Brew a dirty look.

"We'll wait right here, baby," Brew said and eyed over Antonio as if he were dirt. She swallowed hard as she walked ahead with Haley but Antonio trailed behind as Logic said something to him.

"You better wise up fast. I hope you aren't involved with any of those men," Haley said to her.

"They're friends."

"Do I look stupid?" She exhaled.

"Something happened one night. That's all it was."

"Well, don't throw away an opportunity like this and with a man like Antonio. You're going to meet his cousin tomorrow night. You're going to be representing MAX products and fucking around with multiple men is not exactly going to work. You'll be busy advancing your career, and making double if not triple what you make now," Haley said and looked past Alda at the guys then back to her.

"You better think things through and realize what's at stake here. Are you willing to give it up for them? A couple of nights of good sex? You deserve better than that," she said as Antonio approached.

"I'm so sorry about that, Antonio. Brew is protective of me. There was an incident the other night at one of the clubs and he and his friends are still feeling protective."

He looked her over. "Being protective is one thing, acting aggressive, violent is another. Are you certain I can't drive you home? You'll be safe here?"

"Oh God, yes. They're good guys, just a bit protective."

"Hmmm, well, we'll talk tomorrow at the party."

"Yes, and thank you for dinner. For everything."

He pulled her close, her back toward the bar and where the guys were and he kissed her cheek, whispered into her ear.

"You're precious, Alda. We're going to make a good team, and bring MAX Industries to the next level." He winked as he released her but let his hand slide over her ass.

She watched them go and was filled with mixed emotions. What was she supposed to do? Give up a career, a chance at perhaps a committed relationship with Antonio, maybe, and risk it all for four men who didn't do commitments?

She wanted to leave. Just get the hell out of here but she had to go back to the bar, to where the four men stood and get her purse.

The arm wrapped around her waist tight. She gasped.

"Come back over and we'll talk," Train said to her. She damned the sensations she had. It felt so good to feel him pressed against her. Close to her. She didn't have quite the same reaction when Antonio touched her, but she would settle for that, instead of lust. She knew there was nothing more to this.

She swallowed and then turned in his arms. He released her and walked behind her with a hand on her hip. She took position between Royce, and Brew in the space they made and then Logic and Train closed in the gap.

Brew placed his hand over her hip and waist and drew her against his side. He towered over her and the feel of that thick, hard arm against her waist aroused her, damn it.

"Tell me you aren't seeing that dick. That you aren't interested in him."

She looked at him, had to tilt her head back to lock gazes, he was so much taller.

"He isn't any of your business, Brew. You embarrassed me."

His grip tightened and he pulled her closer, his hand squeezed her ass to him. She gasped, placed her hands against his chest.

"It is my fucking business."

"Why is that, Brew?"

"Why the fuck do you think?" he asked through clenched teeth.

"I don't know. It isn't your MO," she snapped at him.

He squinted at her. "What does that mean?"

"Fuck 'em and leave 'em. Isn't that what you call it? What you do? Screw women and don't call them and even tell them not to approach you again."

"What?"

"Yeah, don't think I'm stupid, Brew. I know a woman you screwed. It was part of why I didn't want to risk the one-night stand. I knew what I was getting into. Your non-commitment attitudes. All of you."

He cupped her hair and cheek. "I believe I told you before, during and after my cock was buried deep in your pussy, that this was different."

Her lips parted. His words were so sharp and before she could respond he kissed her. As he released her lips, Logic pulled her toward him and kissed her next. He ran his palm along her ass and squeezed.

"Let's go. Now," Royce commanded.

Logic released her lips but then pulled her through the crowd and out the door. Brew had her purse, Royce and Train looked furious and she was utterly wet. How did they do this to her? How did Brew twist this around and make her want them all over again? How?

* * * *

The moment they got her into the SUV Royce pulled her onto his lap and kissed her hard. Logic drove, Brew was in the passenger seat and Royce and Train were in the back seat with her. Royce ran his hands up her skirt, over her thigh to her hip. She lifted up and rocked on top of him as he plunged his tongue into her mouth.

He felt needy, crazy and jealous. Seeing another man want their woman, touch her hip and even her ass in challenge made him want to beat the fucker up.

Alda moaned into his mouth and he lifted her hip, gripped the thin string of her panties that had to be thongs and rocked his hips upward. He pulled from her mouth.

"I need in," he said to her, and then nipped her breasts in the low cut one piece dress she wore. When he first saw her, he thought she looked hot, sexy, a professional woman.

"How do you do this to me? How?" she asked, breathing heavy.

He gripped her hips under her dress, against her skin tighter and gave her a shake. Teeth clenched, he held her gaze. "You do the same thing to me. Undo my pants, Alda. Take me inside of you now," he demanded. She licked her lips, lifted up and then began to undo his pants. He wiggled from them and she adjusted her position.

Train gripped her hair and pulled her to the side to kiss him as Royce shoved his pants down. He lifted his cock and stroked it. The sound of her panties tearing filled the cabin of the SUV.

He reached out and cupped her breast, her one knee was between his legs and he stroked her cunt as she continued to kiss Train. She was rubbing Train's cock over his pants. Train growled and pulled back.

"Fuck," Train exclaimed.

"You're super fucking wet, baby," Royce said to her and eased a finger along her ass. She lifted up and rocked her hips. He slid a finger into her ass. "Yeah, just like that. You're going to get fucked in every hole tonight, baby. We're going to claim you everywhere, and over and over again until you realize you belong to us," he said to her. Her eyes popped open and she moaned as she came.

He pulled his fingers from her body, brought her over his lap and she took his cock up into her cunt. They both moaned. She gripped his shoulders and he thrust his hips so hard and fast, shoving her downward as he lifted up. Her lips parted, her breasts bounced.

"Pull down your top. I need to see those sexy tits of yours. Come on now. Show them to me," he demanded.

"Oh, Royce. Oh God, you're wild."

"You ain't seen wild yet. Just fucking wait," he said and she eased the material of her dress off her shoulders. Her breasts emerged from her bra. He thrust hard upward.

"Oh," she exclaimed. Train reached over and cupped a breast. Royce watched as Train leaned in and licked the tip.

"All of you will belong to the four of us. Every fucking inch," he exclaimed, gripping her hips and thrusting upward so fast, his thighs were aching.

"Royce, Train, I can't take it. I can't. Oh!" She cried out her release and Royce followed.

"Grrr," he roared.

"Fuck, I can't wait." Train pulled her off of him and onto his lap. Royce moaned and then leaned back to catch his breath.

Train was plunging his tongue into Alda's mouth. Her breasts were bouncing, her thighs exposed.

"I need in," Train said and turned her around. "Grab the middle console now," he ordered, placing her hands on the middle console then undoing his pants and shoving them down. He pulled a shoe off and one leg off his pants. Royce couldn't believe what this woman did to them and how she made them so wild and desperate.

"Train," she said and then Brew turned in his seat, reached out and stroked her breast.

"Beautiful."

Train lifted her dress and pressed it over her back, her bare ass and wet cunt fully exposed to them. He moved in behind her, dick in hand.

"So fucking gorgeous. Hold on tight, baby. We don't have a lot of room but I need you now."

Her hands gripped the console, her thighs were spread wide, her ass full, round and sticking out. Her pussy more bare than he recalled it being the first time they made love. Train shoved into her from behind in one fast thrust.

"Oh!" She moaned, moved a little forward but Train gripped her hips, pulled her back and began to thrust into her. The space was definitely too tight for Train's large frame and height but his brother made do. His ass slammed back against the back seat with every thrust. Royce chuckled to himself. The woman made them all insane.

* * * *

Train gripped Alda's hips and rammed into her. He rocked his hips and wrapped an arm under her waist, cupping one breast and kissing her neck and shoulder. He inhaled her shampoo and absorbed the scents, the sensations, the feel of being inside of her and having her this close. He craved it, needed it all week and she denied them what they wanted and needed.

"Mine. All fucking mine, woman. Every damn inch of you," he growled and she came. He followed, unloading his seed into her womb and still feeling like it wasn't enough. Like it only took the edge off.

He turned her around and pulled her into his arms and against his chest. He fell back against the seat and hugged her tight.

She was breathing heavily, her cheek against his neck and shoulder.

"So fucking good, baby. You make us wild. We don't want to see you with any other men but us. Ever," he told her, caressing her bare ass.

Royce leaned over and kissed her shoulder, ran a hand along her hair and she lifted up to look at him.

"We're here, baby. Get yourself ready. We were apart from you for too many days. We're making up for lost time." Royce kissed her softly and the side door opened.

* * * *

They helped her fix her dress, but she felt so wild walking through the underground garage between Train and Royce and to the private elevator. Once they were inside she locked gazes with Logic and Brew. Both men licked their lips. The doors opened and they ushered her out and to another elevator. Brew punched in a code and she realized it was to the penthouse. Holy shit. They were rich.

The second they walked inside Royce and Train released her and she looked around the place. It was huge and decorated so upscale and manly with bold dark colors, stainless steel appliances, large leather couches and a huge flat screen TV.

"Look at me," Logic said to her. Her heart raced with anticipation. This was crazy, wild, and she couldn't believe she was here with them, letting them take her body like this. She wanted more and more and felt the same way they did. She wanted to make up for lost time and get lost with them. She didn't want to think about her job, the future, only being with these men right now.

Brew held her purse and the yellow envelope in his hands as he stood watching them.

Logic unzipped her dress, and she let her arms hang to the sides as the material fell to the floor. She was naked, only wearing the thin, sheer bra that showed her nipples, but helped to show no lines in the thin, sexy dress she had worn.

He bit his lower lip. Brew was breathing through his nostrils behind her, pulling off his shirt.

"If I ever see that man, any man other than my brothers touch your ass, your body, or try to kiss you, I'm going to kick his fucking ass," Logic warned her. Her lips parted, his intense tone and facial expression, narrowed eyes, heavy breathing made her pussy drip.

"Tell us you want us. That you accept us claiming every part of you tonight," he said to her.

She was shaking, she felt so aroused. She wondered how many women they brought to this luxurious penthouse. How many they seduced and fucked in each of these large rooms and maybe even against the island with the million dollar view in the wall to ceiling glass?

"I don't want to be just another woman you've brought to this penthouse, showing off your wealth and power. I want and need more. It doesn't matter how crazy you make me. Or how needy for each of you to be inside of me. I'm risking everything."

Logic closed the space between them and cupped her hair and head.

"You are the first and only woman we've had in this penthouse. In our home. Don't make me wait any longer. Accept us. We're taking you together."

He stared into her eyes and she knew he would wait, they each would until she accepted them fully.

"Yes. I accept. All of you, together."

He kissed her tenderly, spreading kisses from the corners of her mouth to the center, plunging his tongue deeper, then lifting her up and carrying her through the penthouse.

Logic set her down in the center of the room. He pulled away and undressed quickly. So did the others. She reached back and undid her bra, letting it fall to the rug. Hands were on her everywhere as Brew thrust against her backside, his thick hard cock pressing against the crack.

"Use this. A lot of it," Royce said and she looked toward the bed and the tube of lube there.

Brew gripped her hips while Logic suckled one breast and Train suckled the other. She felt Royce's palm slide along her ass, squeezing her flesh then stroking a finger along her crack. Brew bit gently on a sensitive cord in her neck and shoulder.

"Oh," she moaned, feeling her body go limp, only for the men to hold her upright and feast on her together. Hands spread her thighs, causing her to part her legs then fingers took turns stroking up into her cunt.

"So wet and swollen for cock, aren't you, sweetie?" Train asked her.

"Yes. Oh yes, please," she begged for it.

"You made me wait too long for you, Alda. Too fucking long." He nipped her shoulder then pressed something thick and cold to her asshole as Train lifted her leg and thigh up against his hip on the left side of her. Logic knelt in front of her, held her on the other side stroking her pussy and Royce suckled her breast. Hard.

Brew's finger slid into her asshole all the way as Logic thrust fingers into her cunt slowly.

"Oh, it burns. Oh," she moaned.

"Take slow, easy breaths, Alda. You're so tight, but you want us to claim you, to take you together and make you all ours. You want a cock in this virgin ass. Tell me yes. Tell me yes," Brew demanded and thrust a little faster.

She felt her core tighten and an orgasm hit her so hard she cried out. "Yes! Yes, damn you, yes."

Immediately they pulled fingers from her body and Brew lifted her up, turned her around so he lay on the edge of the bed and she straddled his hips. She felt wild, needy, and as she lowered over his shaft, sunk down on his thick cock, she took in the sight of all his muscles, his tattoos and the demanding, troublemaking terror of a man who turned her on and kissed him wildly. She plunged her tongue into his mouth and ravished him as he had done to her the other night. She rocked her hips and he ran large, warm hands up and down her back, her ass then to her neck. He gripped under her hair and she pulled from his mouth and gasped.

"Relax those muscles, and get that mouth ready for cock," Brew ordered to her just as Logic pressed lube to her asshole. The bed dipped as her ass burned and then began to ease with every stroke.

"Just like that. Nice and easy breaths, and rock those hips. Ride Brew's cock, woman. Take from him what you need," Train said to her as he palmed her ass with one hand and stroked his cock with the other.

"Holy fuck, she looks so hot. She's sucking my fingers in good and tight," Logic stated aloud.

"She's ready. She has to be ready," Brew said through clenched teeth.

"Take me, too, sweetie. Open that sexy mouth and suck my cock," Train said to her. She opened her mouth immediately, never feeling so alive, so sensual and ready for whatever they wanted to do. She licked the tip of Train's thick cock, and then absorbed the taste of him, and the scent of him as she rocked her hips up and down. Hands landed on her hips and then Logic's fingers pulled from her ass just as she felt the orgasm building. She moaned against Train's cock in protest when she felt the thick, bulbous head of Logic's cock press against her asshole then push and nudge into her.

She tightened up.

Smack.

She jerked.

"Ease up and relax those muscles. You're ours, woman. All fucking ours," Royce stated firmly.

She eased her muscles and Logic grunted and complained. "So tight. Too fucking tight." He rocked into her, trying to get in when suddenly she felt the plop and he was inside of her all the way and they all moaned.

"Beautiful. Now claim her together," Royce stated and they all started moving in sync after the direct order. She did her part and sucked and bobbed her head while they filled her with cock and made her theirs, a part of them forever. Tears filled her eyes and hope that this wasn't temporary because she knew she would never be the same again. She couldn't even keep up, the sensations overwhelmed her. Brew gripped her hips and thrust upward. Train stroked into her mouth.

"There. So fucking there," Logic yelled out and came in her ass.

"Move," Royce demanded. Brew and Train chuckled. Train ran his fingers through her hair and spoke to her as Logic eased from her ass.

"So sensual and sexy. Things are going to change, baby. Change so fucking much."

She felt the hands on her shoulders massaging her there and then Royce's cock against her asshole.

"Nice and easy, baby. My turn to claim this ass. We're all going to claim it tonight. All of us," he said and she felt the cool liquid press into her anus and a second later the tip of Royce's thick cock pressed into her asshole.

"Oh man, I can't. Holy fuck, that's incredible," Train said and rocked a little faster. Gripped her hair and she knew he was coming. "Swallow me. All of it," he demanded as he came and she gulped and suckled until he pulled out, moaning.

"Oh," she exclaimed the second Royce shoved into her ass and held still.

"Come on, Alda. Take us. Come on, baby, together," Brew encouraged her and she was gasping for breath, feeling overwhelmed as another orgasm approached. They started to thrust in sync, fucking her ass and pussy then slowing down as if they were making love, marking her, easing inside of her, making a path and paved way that would always be theirs. She could hardly focus as the tears hit her eyes and her vision blurred. "Oh!" She cried out and came.

"Grr." They both growled and pumped into her then came at the same time.

Royce kissed her shoulders and spine as he eased out of her ass. She lay flat against Brew's chest, his hands caressing her everywhere and then his mouth and lips kissed her cheeks and jaw. He eased her to the side, slid from her cunt and then spread more kisses along her breast and neck. Train raised her arms up above her head as Logic and he washed her up and then kissed her from palms to toes, tickling her.

* * * *

Train traced along the cleavage of Alda's breasts as she lay on the bed. Royce held her wrists above her head, kissing her other breast. Brew and Logic sat in large cushioned chairs at the edge of the bed, watching them and resting. He looked at the light scratch on her hip healing quickly and his chest tightened, remembering that night. He traced her tattoo and she inhaled, tilting her hips up. He glanced back at her watching him, eyes glazed over with desire, body naked to their eyes, their touch.

"So tell us about Antonio and your so-called business meetings with him."

She tightened up and Royce gripped her wrists and leaned closer to her lips.

"Never lie to us. Remember that."

"And you?" she retorted quickly.

"Will be honest with you," he said and then kissed her lips. Royce pulled back and Train continued to caress her skin and trace the tattoo.

"There's a lot going on at work," she whispered.

"That involves him and you meeting for dinner, having an intimate drink at bars?" Brew asked from the edge of the bed.

"Not intimate."

"Don't. I saw his hand on your ass," Brew stated and sat up, rested his elbows on his knees, his legs apart and stared at her body.

"He touched your hair tonight. Gazed into your eyes and kept a hand on you like you belonged to him. Hell, he even pulled you close as if to protect you from us," Logic told her.

"I've been with him all week."

"What?" Train asked, stopping what he was doing.

"Not with him, with him. Just at work, at the studio, and out to dinner. There's so much happening right now."

"That's why you made up reasons to avoid getting together with us?" Royce asked, releasing her wrists and sitting up.

"You had excuses, too," she countered.

"If you want to call trying to track down this fucking asshole drug dealer making the pills that could have gotten you and Alessa gang raped, sure," Brew raised his voice at her.

She lifted up, leaning on her elbows. "That's what you've been doing? Not avoiding me, running from a one-night stand?" she asked, looking and sounding shocked.

"One-night stand? Is that what you thought of our first night together?" Logic asked her.

"I did, because Royce and Brew were gone when I woke up and Train and Logic didn't even ask for breakfast or act like they wanted to stay. They were like take a shower or soak, and then just standing there when I walked into the room. It was awkward," she told them.

"Honey, we never ever stayed at a woman's place, nor took the same woman together," Royce told her.

"What? No. No way, not with your reputations," she said and sat up, pulled the covers up to cover her body.

"Don't believe everything you've heard about us. Women, people talk and make shit up," Logic said to her.

"We're getting off track here. Back to Antonio and the fact the man wants you in his bed. What are you going to do about him?" Brew asked.

She stared at Brew.

"What are you proposing?" she asked him.

"Proposing?" Brew asked.

"Sure. You're telling me the other night was not a one-night stand. I'm assuming tonight isn't either since I did let you make love to me together and I've never let any man do to me what the four of you have, so I think it's safe to say I am hoping there's more to this than just sex."

Royce caressed her thigh.

"This is new to us, too. We've never had a woman come over to our penthouse, never mind sleep in my bed or any bed," Royce said to her. Obviously this was his room.

Train could see her expression like she was expecting more than that.

"We need time to adjust to this, too," Train said to her.

"As I do, too," she said.

Train wanted to tell her to stay away from other men, and from this Antonio guy, but how could he? They all needed to be on board with this and the reason why she was pissed at them was because they pushed her away and they were still trying to get over these new emotions.

"Back to Antonio. What's going on with work and changes?" Royce asked her this time.

"The company is expanding and looking to promote overseas one product at a time," she said to them.

"Overseas?" Logic asked.

"Yes, and Antonio, his cousin and the company they have are negotiating terms of importing and exporting services for MAX Industries. I had to do a lot of prep work for this potential new position they're offering me," she said to them.

"What new position?" Train asked.

"What prep work?" Brew asked and she lowered her eyes and her cheeks flushed.

"They want me to be the image, the face of the cosmetic line. I had to go to the salon, get the works done, then to the studio for a shoot all day Tuesday, the proofs are over there if you want to see them," she said and pointed to the dresser where they had placed her purse and the yellow folder earlier. Logic walked over and opened the file. He whistled.

"Let me see," Brew stated and Logic showed him a picture and then placed the folder onto the bed. They spread them out, looking at Alda posing, some close ups, some far away. She was dressed professionally yet sexy, with her cleavage showing. Train noticed one particular picture where she leaned against a square cube that had makeup products on it, her hand on her waist, her brown hair flowing and a tight black dress that showed how well-endowed she was, and the roundness of her breasts, tan legs crossed, and sexy as damn hell.

"Holy fuck, this is a hot shot," Royce said and held that picture up.

"So Antonio was with you for this shoot and all these pictures?" Brew asked her as Logic gathered up the shots and stared at the one they each thought was the sexiest.

"He picked the best shot. Along with Maxwell and Haley, and of course the photographers."

Brew climbed up the bed. He pushed the covers from her body and spread her thighs, climbing between her legs.

"That dick got to see you posing all sexy, and even looked at photos with you to decide the best ones? Did he have his hands on your ass as you looked?" he asked, raising his voice.

"No, Brew. He was very professional, and nice. I think he's a very nice guy."

"Nice enough to sleep with?" he asked.

She shook her head.

"I don't like him and I don't trust him. He wants what's ours. Limit your alone time with him and no more lunch dates," he told her then pulled her down by her ankles before pressing between her legs and kissing her.

Train looked at Royce and Logic. He didn't like the feeling he had. Jealousy, uncertainty filled his heart and that wasn't like him or his brothers at all. They were rock solid men with steel hearts. Alda was perfection and then some. Could they make a real commitment to her, or was she right? Was it just lust, a super strong attraction that eventually would die out? He didn't think so, because for the first time in Train's life, he wanted a woman for more than just her body, and temporarily. He wanted Alda entirely, and the thought of her with any other man besides his brothers made him see red. It was a lot to process, but they had time. It was only a week, not quite since they first had sex. In another week they could re-evaluate their feelings and the next steps. Maybe.

Chapter 8

"How are things coming along with that company? Can you get the deal signed so we can increase supply?" Salento Sorenno asked Antonio over the phone.

"It's taking some time. I don't think we should rush this, Salento."

"I want to make the money fast and start this operation going."

"I understand that, but Tatum and I need to ensure that this plan is foolproof. We're working with manufacturers now to see how we can smuggle the product in and make it undetectable."

"By breaking it down to powder form and placing it into the makeup palettes. Once they hit the states you can break them down into capsules carefully. Every bit counts of that stuff," Salento stated.

"You don't need to tell me since we created it. The fewer people who know about this operation, the better," Antonio replied.

"Agreed. Now, about the supply I have now. It isn't enough. I've got people offering to pay double the price. I have a list."

"What we gave you needs to suffice or we could risk getting busted," Antonio told Salento.

"You don't understand, Antonio. It's over a million profit. A million just from this small amount you got me. I want more."

"I thought the plan was to work out international shipment and getting through customs so we can hit overseas?"

"You're worried about getting caught, why not keep things local, within the US. Hell, Antonio, we're distributing pill by pill here in NY and making millions. You can take your time getting things ready with the overseas situation and that company you want to use to hide the product. That takes some pressure off you and Tatum, doesn't it? Maybe leaves time for other things."

Antonio thought about that a moment. There really was no need to rush. After seeing the men's reactions to Alda tonight he was concerned about possessing her. Tatum was meeting her tomorrow night at the party. Antonio knew Tatum wouldn't be patient. He would give him days, maybe a few dinners or lunch meetings with Alda before he would want her in his bed. Their bed.

"I'll let you know about additional product. You be sure that you put good people in charge of distributing that and we get top fucking dollar. You can get me the money tomorrow night at the event at the Grand Marquis."

"Excellent. I will take care of it, and have the product sold and money in hand within twenty-four hours," Salento Sorenno told Antonio and then Antonio ended the call.

He leaned back in his chair, his tie off, his collar undone and he thought about this evening, about the possessive, protective way those four men acted with Alda. Could they have feelings for her? Want her? All four? It was possible. He felt the anger pool in his gut. She was his, and Tatum's. He knew the moment he saw her, spoke to her, that she was special and that she could finally be the woman Tatum was looking for. The one they could share. He didn't want to think about her being with other men. He had to be realistic though. She was a beauty, and she was quite independent, enjoyed the night life with friends, and was no virgin. Hell, it could be positive that she could handle more than one man in bed. Tatum had particular tastes and a woman would need to be strong, submissive at the same time in order to handle it.

They left with her. Probably brought her home, maybe they were fucking her right now.

He felt his blood pressure rise, and heat encase his body. He downed the brandy and then put the glass down. He needed to keep her busy, keep her away from those men and instead remain with him and Tatum as much as possible. If Tatum found out she was with other men his cousin may not go so gentle on her. There may not be time for several dinners and courting her. He may need to rush things along more quickly. Antonio needed a plan. A place to take her and force those other men from her life, from her mind, and from ever touching or possessing her body again. He tapped his chin. Yes, he needed a plan. A good one, and when the time came he could make the move, whisk her away, and those assholes would no longer be a threat, but a memory of what tried to stand in his and Tatum's way, but couldn't.

* * * *

Alda sat on the couch in her robe after taking a shower and drying her hair. She tucked her feet under her bottom as the guys made breakfast, and enough to feed an army. Watching them, and how big they all were and filled with muscles, they kind of were an army and definitely had salacious appetites. Especially for her.

She still didn't know what would come of this relationship, or if it really was one. Now that they weren't touching her, making love to her, she was feeling wary again on whether this could work, and also about her job and the current potential opportunity. Haley was pretty firm in her evaluation of the situation last night and where Alda should focus. On her profession and not some one-night stand, or sexual fantasy that may last a short period of time. How would it look if the representative of a high-end cosmetic line was involved in a ménage with four men? Not a committed relationship, but some taboo relationship frowned upon by so many in society. How would her family react? Her cousins, who knew who these men were, who they worked with and were connected to, and certainly knew their reputations with women. Was she being naïve? Were Royce, Brew, Logic, and Train being realistic, too, or were they all, her included, caught up in the sensations, the lust, the connection between them that they couldn't see what eventually would come? Separation.

As she looked at them, and Logic turned, giving her a wink, then Royce walked by and caressed her shoulder then gave it a squeeze and she smiled at him, she felt like this was perfect. Like they truly cared about her and this could maybe work. Maybe not forever, but because it felt so good, perhaps she could hold on to them for as long as she could? Then she thought about the way they avoided discussing past today, past making love, and sharing anything personal about them. She asked a simple question, something that could ease her fears and her mind with these complex and hardened men. She asked them to tell her something personal about them. Something others didn't know. She wasn't asking for a marriage proposal or to know if they ever killed anyone, or some sort of dark secret, she just wanted to know if they had parents, family maybe, where they grew up, or if they preferred football over hockey or baseball, or maybe NASCAR or golf, something that told her a little bit about them on a personal level. Instead they cut her off. Kissed her, made love to her again, or simply turned the conversation around to focus on her, and get more personal information on her. They were distrusting, private, intimidating men, yet somehow they penetrated her heart and made her like them way too much to be treated like they felt so little for her.

She still wondered if it was just sex for them, but great sex, like none they had with another woman before and perhaps that was what made them hang on instead of push her away entirely like they seemed to do with other women.

Was that supposed to make her feel special, and like she was the one needing to sacrifice everything for them while they still went on doing what they did? She would be stupid to believe that Haley would accept this. That Maxwell would and Antonio, too. She would lose this new position as the cover model, the representative of the makeup product line. For them, could she give it up when they were offering nothing in return, no indication of commitment, just ride it while it lasted? Her chest tightened and her gut clenched. Tears filled her eyes and she closed them and laid her head down on the cushion on the couch, watching them. Brew was looking at the laptop. Royce was doing something with his phone. Texting, reading messages or e-mails and Logic and Train were cooking breakfast. They talked about what they needed to do today, and how crazy of a weekend it would be working at Oliva and going by Club Empire Saturday night.

"So how is next week for you guys?" she asked, and only Royce looked at her.

"Busy as damn hell," he replied and started talking about some meetings and business things but nothing specific and she knew they wouldn't tell her anything and it needed to remain private. In her head she saw the week go by in a flash.

"We'll call you and maybe stop in after work one night, or you can give us a key to your place and one of us if not all of us can sneak in and spend some time with you," Brew suggested.

A booty call in the middle of the night? She would be their guaranteed sex toy, conveniently available in the middle of the night after they spent hours at their clubs, surrounded by women drooling over them, touching them, arousing them only for them to come to her place and fuck her for relief? This didn't sound like the relationships her friends had with their made men. She felt insulted, hurt, pissed, and then quickly processed everything and replied as she sat up.

"I have a busy week, too, starting tonight and over the weekend. This is new for all of us. Taking our time would be wise, so no key to my place. Is that coffee ready yet?" she asked, putting on her sexy smile and walking into their kitchen and by Logic and Train. Train pulled her close and looked at the gap in the robe they gave her.

"We'll get together Sunday night. Okay?" he said and then kissed her lips and ran his hand over her ass. She pressed her palms to his chest as he held the spatula in one hand and flipped the pancakes. He wasn't even looking at her, yet he was touching her and it affected her entire body. It wasn't fair. Not fair at all.

She slipped from his arms and busied herself with coffee, offering them some too and then passing out the mugs after fixing them like they wanted. She took hers black, hoping the bitterness would alleviate the anger, the hurt and the sickness in her gut. Sambuca would have done a better job burning her throat and her emotions away. She closed her eyes and then willed herself to hold in the tears and get through breakfast, then she would ask them to get her home so she could prepare for tonight and decide what was best for her and her future, and what she really felt she deserved. She wanted to be cared for, loved, respected and protected. She didn't want to feel used, meaningless, or temporary, and that was what she was feeling right now and it wasn't good at all.

Chapter 9

"She isn't answering my text," Train said to Logic.

"Alda is at a party, more than likely talking business and her phone is in her purse. She'll text like we told her," Logic replied.

Train looked at Royce and Brew. They were both extra snappy tonight. Earlier they had discovered the possibility of a connection with this new drug and Salento Sorenno. Not a very nice guy, and one involved with pretty bad shit. He was out of Connecticut, but had his hands on everything from street drugs to prostitution. Royce and Brew had dealings with him in the past.

Dominick, Giuseppe, and Andreas bought out the building next door to where Oliva now was. They owned the block of apartment buildings, store fronts along with Royce and Brew. At the time Train and Logic had money tied up in their own businesses of storage facilities and distribution centers for liquors and beers that provided products to the surrounding bars and restaurants in the area. They each had their own money, own income and also shared businesses together.

They also cut deals with their friends Lenox, Cobra, Roman, Ziek and even Jack, Turbo, Covan, and Harley to be silent partners in it all. They were trustworthy and good friends.

Train swallowed hard, unable to get the bad feeling out of his gut. He didn't like having Alda out of his sight. Her behavior was off this morning as they talked about their busy weeks. He had the feeling that she might have been hurt, or insulted by them not being able to get together constantly. They didn't exactly offer her a commitment, verbally or other than asking for a key to her place. That was pretty serious. They never even dated one woman or maintained interest in one, but with Alda everything was different.

He knew his brothers were feeling the connection, the potential of seriousness this relationship could have. They were being stubborn and fighting it, and Train couldn't help but worry that it could cause Alda to not trust them, and maybe even keep her distance and put up walls. They had a lot to work on in regards to making a commitment solely to her, making her feel special and cared for, and not just a lover.

His phone went off. He glanced at it and the relief he felt at seeing it was a response from Alda surprised him. He read the text and squinted.

Super crowded and loud in here. I can't talk now. Have a good night. I'll touch base during the week.

"Touch base during the week? What the fuck does that mean?" he said aloud.

"What is it?" Logic asked. He showed him her text.

"That doesn't sound good."

"No shit."

"We'll have to handle it later, Royce is waving us over, Dominick needs our help again." Train nodded and put his phone on the clip on his hip, then followed Logic. He wasn't happy. Hell, he was pissed off and concerned. Was she blowing him off? Them off? He couldn't help but feel like he and his brothers were screwing this up. He needed to talk to them. They had to figure out where they stood in this relationship and admit to Alda what they were all feeling. No one liked to be vulnerable and in their line of business vulnerability got people killed. This was not business though, and if they weren't honest with Alda, they could lose her completely.

* * * *

Alda felt the arm go around her waist and lips against her bare shoulder. The off the shoulder dress accentuated her large breasts and trim waist. It was long, to the floor, but the slit up the side made it look sexy and classy. It was in a deep burgundy red and she wore matching high heels.

She tightened and then exhaled.

"Something wrong?" Antonio asked and then shifted to face her, letting his large warm hand caress along her waist. He didn't remove it as he stared down into her eyes. She knew she looked emotional.

He narrowed his eyes. "What is it?"

She shook her head and put the phone in her clutch. "Nothing. I'm good. Are you enjoying the party?" she asked him. He stared at her, looking so fierce, seasoned, experienced. She bet he had a lot of women just as Brew, Royce, Logic, and Train did. Maybe she was being foolish and blowing their resistance, their noncommitment to her out of proportion? Should she give them time as if they needed to adjust or was she being stupid? They may never adjust and just think, she would bend for them and change her life for them while they kept doing their thing and she kept worrying about whom they might cheat on her with.

Antonio's palm cupped her cheek and she looked at him, teary eyed.

"You're sad, hurt, and I can't help but think that it has something to do with those men from the other night. You're a beautiful, professional woman who deserves to be catered to, cared for, put first and cherished. Not taken for granted." His words hit her hard. That was exactly what she was feeling. For granted, like she would be there for them to screw, to pleasure and give pleasure while they went about their lives, not even committing to solely her. Did she not trust them?

"Oh, sweet Alda." He pulled her into his arms and walked her out of the crowded room and toward the hallways and private enclave. She wiped her eyes and took a deep breath then exhaled as he caressed her and held her close. He felt big, muscular, and his cologne appealing.

"I'm sorry, Antonio. This is so unprofessional of me. I'm embarrassed," she said and pulled back. He kept his hands on her hips and then reached up and stroked her cheek.

"Don't apologize for hurting, and feeling used. Men like that are a dime a dozen, out to get what they want, to take and take but not give in return. You're too beautiful, too special, Alda, for that kind of treatment. You have a lot going on in your career. Your future is so bright, I'd hate for you to throw it all away on a fling, on a dead end avenue. Don't let them do that to you," he said to her.

"I feel so confused."

He squinted at her and brushed his thumb along her lower lip.

"You're not confused when we're together, are you? I mean, I know I'm one man, and perhaps can't compete with men a little younger like they are, but my experiences, being seasoned, my mistakes and successes help me to see and appreciate a woman like you. I would not take you for granted, Alda. With me you would know where I stand. You would come first. Your happiness would be my life's work," he said to her and gave a soft smile, stroking her cheek. She couldn't help but to smile and then sniffle.

"You are gorgeous when you're smiling and happy. This last week I didn't see much smiling and I don't like it."

"I appreciate the compliments, Antonio, I do. I'll get through this and figure it out."

"There's not much to figure out, Alda. I can make you happy, make you smile, show you how special you actually are instead of using you for what I want. They're using you, plain and simple. How can four men stay faithful to one woman when they've obviously never committed to one ever?"

She nodded. "You're right. I keep thinking the same thing."

"If it's a worry about your reputation now that you've been with four men, I'm willing to put that aside and pretend it never happened.

Let me show you how a real man treats a woman he cares for deeply and can commit to."

He clenched her chin, she tightened only a moment, her mind frazzled at her thoughts, at Antonio's words and actions and then his lips were over hers and he kissed her gently, passionately. She let him, and she decided she truly needed to analyze what was best for her, especially since it seemed the only other person looking out for Alda was Antonio.

* * * *

Antonio watched Alda laughing along with Tatum. They hit it off immediately, his cousin a character and very suave and charismatic with Alda. It just solidified the fact that she was definitely meant to be with them. Tatum looked at him several times and he knew that he wanted her with them in bed tonight. It was too soon. So much happened here, and he needed to make sure she didn't have second thoughts and still wanted to be with those four men.

"I hadn't expected them to get along so well," Haley whispered to Antonio.

"It's fate, I suppose."

"What about those men?" Haley asked.

"I'm working on that. Your assistance could be helpful. Make sure you get pictures of us together. I want them all over the place," he said and Haley signaled the photographer as Antonio walked over to Alda and placed his hand on her hip. She smiled up at him and one look at Tatum and he couldn't help but feel smug.

"I will not allow you to keep her to yourself, cousin. Alda is way too special," Tatum said and kissed her cheek. She blushed.

"You're too sweet, Tatum, and have such a wonderful personality. How come Antonio hasn't brought you along to the meetings and things all week?" she asked.

"I was feeling a little under the weather from traveling," he said and went about explaining to her about his jet lag and about the multiple trips overseas with business. Antonio pressed a kiss to her head.

"You would love it, Alda. You should come with us the next time we head to Paris or Germany. We can show her all the best restaurants and that little cottage you adore so much, Antonio," Tatum said.

"A cottage?" she asked.

"Oh yes, it's a small little place located on a vineyard. That's sacred ground to Antonio. His retreat, and place to get away from it all."

Her eyes widened. "It sounds lovely. I'm sure it must be hard to get time off when you're running multiple businesses and flying overseas and back and forth to the States," she said.

"Picture," the photographer stated, interrupting them and Tatum and Antonio both pressed close to Alda and held her.

"It can be, perhaps you would like to see it in person and enjoy it with us?" he whispered to her.

"She would love the gardens, and the vineyard where they make the wine and we can sample some," Tatum said and she glanced at him. Tatum kissed her neck and Antonio held her possessively. These pictures were going to be perfect.

Alda pressed back.

"I've never been out of the country before. I'm always so busy working and I'm sure this new position won't give me much free time," she said and stepped away from them.

Antonio took her hand and pulled her close. He whispered to her. "We are not them. Those men who used you, who played with your emotions and heart."

"No, Antonio, that's not what happened."

"Sure it is. If it meant something then they wouldn't be making you sad, or causing tears like earlier."

"What's this all about?" Tatum asked. Antonio looked at him and pulled Alda closer.

"She's been hurt by four men. They played with her heart, tricked her, and she's confused about her feelings now because she's so kind and sweet...unsuspecting of such cruelty." He stroked her jaw and tilted her chin up toward him. Tatum pressed up against her back and held her hips.

"My cousin and I are wise men, experienced, knowing what we want, and more importantly we don't play games. A relationship with us would last forever, Alda. We could travel together, work on this new business venture together, and make you happy, not sad."

"Antonio, it isn't that simple. I need time to process everything. I feel raw right now and confused."

"They've done that, too. Made you second guess yourself, and minimize the importance of what you want and need in life. Trust us, Alda. We'll give you time, but don't fall for their lies."

Chapter 10

Alda had to wake up very early the next morning to make it to the studio. A good while after lunch Giada called her.

"Hello."

"How was last night?" Giada asked.

"It was amazing. Such a wonderful event. I was so tired this morning but had to be at the studio early. I'm on my second cup of coffee."

"Well, did you see the front cover of the Manhattan entertainment section?"

"No, I didn't look, why?"

"Well, that event you were at and your company's new product line is featured with you and two very handsome, sexy older men sandwiching you between them. Who the hell are they and what happened with you, Brew, Royce, Logic, and Train?" Giada asked her.

"Oh God, the front cover of the section. How is the picture really?"

"Oh, you look incredible, as do the two sexy hunks, but it is provocative. I mean, I can't totally tell if the one guy's hand is on your ass or not, but they both have a possessive hand over your hips and belly. Sexy indeed. So what's the deal? I have to hear this," Giada asked.

"Well, I have about fifteen minutes. I was going to call you when I got a chance and ask your advice, but…"

"But you did the two sexy guys last night and there hasn't been time?"

"No! Of course not, how could I do that after what I shared with Brew, Royce, Train, and Logic?"

"I don't know. The picture makes me question you a lot. Just wait until the guys see it and find out."

"What are the chances that they read the entertainment section?" Alda asked.

"My men saw it and they weren't happy at all," Giada stated.

"So that's why you're really calling me? To get info for them? That's what I was afraid of. I'm trying not to be influenced by outside sources. I mean, Haley is saying one thing and about my image and then you guys are all like go for it and ride it while it lasts, but I'm confused. I don't want to be their booty call woman. I mean, they asked me for a fucking key to my apartment so they can sneak in in the middle of the night if they're working late to get some. Really? Who asks for that? We haven't even gone on a date, I know nothing but what everyone else knows about them and when I asked for something personal they changed the subject."

Alda went on and on about what transpired in the last couple of days. Giada listened and gasped a few times, added her comments.

"No wonder you're so confused. I don't like that Haley lady. She's up to something."

"Well, Giada, I was thinking the same thing last night. She was extra pushy for me not to get involved with Antonio and Tatum, but yet she told me how frowned upon it would be if I was involved in a ménage with four men when I was set to be the cover model for MAX cosmetics."

"You really are in a jam. No wonder you're so upset with those four idiots. They are so used to being on guard, acting tough and macho that they're pushing you away and into two other men's arms. I understand your confusion, Alda. I do, but I have to be honest here, I have never seen Train, Logic, Royce, and Brew act like this. I think, no, I know they care about you. A lot. It's got to be a first for them. Not that I'm saying they're handling it right, but in all relationships there has to be honesty and communication. In a ménage there must be trust. If that trust is betrayed then it's doomed to fail."

"So you're saying I betrayed them by not giving them time to process how they feel about me? Am I supposed to stand back, give up my career, my life, my independence and just wait and see if they commit or they bail? I have so much lying on the line here and they don't. If this relationship fails they move on, screwing who they want when they want. I'm used goods. I lose my job, this new position and any chance at landing something else in this field because shit like this travels."

"You need to calm down. I'm not saying any of that. You didn't sleep with them, right?" Giada asked.

"Of course not."

"Then there is still time. Talk to Train, Logic, Brew and Royce. Tell them what you're feeling, explain what it is you need from them in order to give them a chance."

"And what about work?"

"Honey, if they don't give you the position because you are in love with four men then it's their loss. Like I said, that Haley woman seems untrustworthy and Antonio and Tatum could be up to something, too. Are you really willing to take such a chance on strangers instead of four men who have been around you for at least a year, are good friends with all your friends, and practically family? Seriously? We'd all beat their assess for hurting you," Giada stated.

Alda chuckled and wiped the tears from her eyes.

"I better get going. I have a few more hours of this then I need to hail a cab home. Tomorrow I'm sleeping in."

"Tonight, we're meeting at Empire, remember?"

"Then I'd better cut out of here early and take a nap. I'm going to need it."

Giada laughed.

"I hope it all works out. I'll be here if you need to talk, but just know if you try to text the guys and cut off them finding out about that picture or any others that may be floating around, they're all in some kind of meeting. I think they're getting closer to finding out who is selling that drug Alessa was given," Giada told her.

"I hope they do find out who it is and stop them. The thought of what could have happened scares me."

"It scares all of us and any unknowing female out there just having a fun night out with friends. Kind of like what we all enjoyed doing for so long."

"I know. Lucky we're always looking out for one another," Alda said.

"Lucky we're all close-knit with made men. Single or not, you, Donata, any of our friends are protected. These men are our families and men we can trust. No doubt about that," Giada said.

Alda agreed and then ended the call.

* * * *

"You want to make some good money, stick with me, C.J., Brendan and I got into something big. It was a little risky but worth it," Fogerty told C.J.

They were standing by the back door of some warehouse in Hoboken. "What the hell are we doing here, and why couldn't you explain what this was about on the way here?" C.J. asked.

"Because I didn't want you freaking out. Now that you're here, you're part of it."

C.J, swallowed hard. He didn't like the sound of this, but he noticed Fogerty was really bringing in the money lately. A lot of it.

"So what's the deal then? I'm here," C.J. said to him.

"Okay, you can't tell a soul. There is this new drug. People are paying big bucks for it. Five hundred a pill."

"What? Who would be stupid enough to do that?" C.J. asked.

"Not stupid, it's worth it and then some. It's like a date rape drug, except the woman doesn't remember a damn thing. It makes them act drunk, and they don't remember a thing that's going on so the guy or guys get away with doing whatever they want to them."

"That's fucked up."

"Yeah, well, at five hundred a pop, we get paid to not only pick this stuff up at non-disclosed locations but I got in on dealing it out, too. I did my first few deliveries this week and tonight I have a bunch. The guy pays me a grand a night."

"I'm surprised a man like Lou Carvetti who does some work for the Garlitto family would be into this kind of drug. I mean, I know they own routes and shit, but this drug sounds dangerous and a cop magnet."

"First of all, Carvetti doesn't know and therefore neither does Garlitto. This is done under the radar and only select individuals can purchase this stuff. They have to have an in."

"So what you're saying is you're using your abilities and the locations where Carvetti does his deals to also do separate deals with this guy and this drug behind Garlitto's back?" C.J asked.

"Pretty much, but they won't care even if they find out because I've put money aside to make them forget about it. If they approach me on it I have a payoff. It will all work out, plus this guy's plan is to only distribute small batches and for a short period of time. I think they're afraid of the same thing, a demand and then sending up smoke signals of where the shit is coming from."

"How can you even look at these guys who come to buy the drugs and not think what a bunch of fucking loser dirtbags? They need a drug to get some woman into bed."

"I don't see their faces and I don't give a fuck. If you start thinking like that and even have morals or question why people use drugs instead of exploit them for whatever money you can get out of them then you're in the wrong business, C.J. You should become a fucking good Samaritan or a fucking moron working eighty hours a week and live in the fucking ghetto."

C.J. went to respond but then they heard the door unlock and Fogerty tap his side. "I do all the talking. You are here to carry the duffel bag of shit."

C.J. looked at the guy. He eyed him over and then Fogerty.

As the deal went down C.J. had a bad feeling. It wouldn't be smart to double-cross anyone in the Garlitto family, or even Lou Carvetti. Maybe he should cut his losses and get out before he got caught up in something he wasn't ready to go to jail for?

* * * *

"What the fuck?" Brew yelled and threw the newspaper down onto the table. They had all seen it, even went online and found other pictures of Alda in between the two men.

"Calm down," Royce said very calmly, but he didn't look calm to Brew. Royce looked angry. Train had his arms crossed in front of his chest and was breathing through his nostrils, and Logic just stood there speechless, blank.

"Just because there are pictures of them together doesn't mean she went home with them last night. We texted her. She said she was home," Logic stated.

"She could have lied. We didn't go by her place and see for ourselves," Brew raged.

"That isn't the kind of woman she is," Train said to them.

"Really? Like you know what kind of fucking woman she is? She played us. We...got played," Brew said and threw his hands up in the air.

"That's what your rage is about? Really, Brew? Be fucking truthful. You like her a lot. You want her to be solely ours and no one else's but what did you do? What did we all do? Acted like fucktards. We didn't let her know that we were feeling insecure, vulnerable, and never had feelings like this for a woman before," Train said to him.

"Pussies? You think we needed to act like fucking pussies and that would have kept her from straying from us with these two rich dicks?" He slammed his finger down on the paper as he leaned over it.

"We finally found a woman we all want, desire, that turns us on and drives us wild and she just dropped us for these two men and you think it's because they acted like pussies and comforted her, made her promises of commitments and dates, movies night and candy and we acted like the tough fucking made men we are?" Brew yelled.

"That's exactly what happened," Logic said.

They were all quiet and Brew couldn't stand still. He was pacing with his hands on his hips. Since seeing that paper this morning and finding out from the guys, from Turbo and his team, from Dominick, Andreas and Giuseppe and the others as they asked what the fuck they did to push her away, Brew was fuming mad. He also felt hurt, insulted, and like he had been tricked. Then he thought about that guy, Antonio.

"You know, the other night that dick pulled her closer as if he was protecting her from us. He can't be so fucking stupid that he didn't see our guns. He wanted Alda that night, was probably working on seducing her. Last night he made another move and brought reinforcements. The other douchebag," Brew said to them, squinting his eyes and thinking about it.

"You're right. He was pompous and acted like we didn't intimidate him but maybe his focus was solely on Alda and letting her see he would protect her," Logic said.

"Then we took her home. We made love to her, and in the morning when she was asking us to tell her something personal about ourselves, we blew it off and changed the subject and acted like we weren't sure what day this week we could see her again," Train said.

"We asked her for a key to her place. She probably thought we would show up in the middle of the night for sex," Logic said.

"What are we saying here? It sounds a hell of a lot like we want to make a full commitment to Alda. That we want her to be our woman, and that we don't want any other women, only her and we don't want her to be with any other men but us. We basically want a fucking girlfriend," Royce said, sounding shocked.

"First, she's going over my knee and getting her ass spanked for letting two other guys kiss her, touch her, and tell her fucking lies to push us away. Then, we're going to show her exactly how much she means to us," Brew stated firmly and walked over to the mirror to recheck his tie and suit jacket. They were going to Club Empire. All their friends and Alda were going to be there.

"If she accepts talking to us," Logic said.

"Accepts it? The woman better not give me any hell or I'll toss her ass over my shoulder and bring her home kicking and screaming, I don't care. She's our woman. I've never, never, felt like this before and neither have any of you. She's ours, and I'm not giving her up without a fight. Let's go," Brew said.

Train slapped his hands together and rubbed them.

"Damn, her ass is going to be nice and pink."

Royce and Logic chuckled.

"I suggest not throwing her over your shoulder immediately. Maybe try something more discrete," Royce said, teasing Brew.

"We're in this together. If that's what it takes to get her to talk to us and explain what went wrong in the last forty some odd hours, then I'm all for barbaric rituals and acting like cavemen," Logic added, and they laughed as they headed out to the SUV.

"Whatever happens, remember we hurt her, made her distrust us, and helped to push her into those men's arms last night. That can never happen again," Royce said.

"We'll get her back. I won't take no for an answer," Brew said.

* * * *

"They aren't here yet," Giada said to Alda as she greeted her hello. Dominick and Giuseppe said hello too and she could tell they were looking at her differently.

"How was your party last night? Looked like a big deal," Giuseppe said to her.

"Very funny, Giuseppe. She didn't hook up with the two guys. Leave her be," Giada said and then gasped as Dominick gave Giada's ass a smack.

"Watch it," he warned. Alda snickered.

"So, the party, how was it?" Gisella asked, standing between Fedarro and Collin.

"Enlightening, I suppose," Alda stated and pulled off her coat.

Giada whistled.

"You look amazing."

Alda debated on what to wear for a good two hours, then when Antonio called and invited her to a cocktail party at some big shot business guy's penthouse uptown, she figured she better wear something amazing, in case things didn't work out here at Club Empire and she needed to have a plan B. She kind of wondered why she was bothering. She was here because of the conversation with Giada today.

"That dress is stunning and sexy, where did you get it and in that deep burgundy color?" Gisella asked.

"Thank you. I've had it for a while. I was invited to a cocktail party uptown later tonight," she said and Collin handed her a pomegranate martini.

"Thank you, Collin," she said and took a sip.

"A cocktail party? Where at?" Gisella asked.

"Near Times Square. I don't exactly know the address, Antonio was going to send a car for me wherever I am if I decided to go," she said.

"A car for you? Is he super rich or what?" Giada asked.

"I guess pretty well off. He owns multiple homes. One in Naples, Italy, Some small town in Germany, and somewhere else. I'm not sure. It's what I picked up on in conversation during the week with business affairs and things," she told them.

"Well, who was the other guy?" Gisella asked.

"That's Antonio's cousin, Tatum."

"Hot," Gisella said.

"Ouch," she exclaimed as Fedarro did something to her backside, maybe pinched it.

"What? I was just complimenting the men Alda is working with, that's all," she said and Alda felt uncomfortable talking about the guys in front of Brew, Royce, Logic, and Train's friends.

"How is Alessa doing? She isn't coming, right?" Alda asked.

"No, she didn't want to leave her place. Her cousins are with her," Gisella said to her.

"I feel so badly for her. I wish there was more I could do, but I guess it will take time," Alda said.

Giada's eyes widened and then she nodded toward the doorway. Alda looked and locked gazes with Brew first. All four men walked into the place looking important, and ready for action. When a couple of blondes approached, calling Brew and Royce by name and touching them, Alda's gut ached and she turned away.

"Alda, they got rid of the women," Giada said to her.

Alda shook her head.

"This is stupid. I shouldn't have come. I think I'm going to head to that cocktail party," Alda said.

"Wait, Alda, just give them a chance," Collin said to her, shocking her and apparently Gisella as her eyes widened and then she hugged Collin's arms.

"That's an order," Gisella added and then pulled Collin along. Dominick and the guys took Giada's hands and left Alda alone for about five seconds. She faced the bar and a moment later one thick strong arm wrapped around her waist, instantly making that empty feeling disappear and she had to refocus as to not lean back into Royce and sigh in pleasure.

"You are in a lot of trouble, wearing a sexy dress like this and standing alone at the bar," he said and kissed her neck. She turned to face him.

"I don't mind being alone. In fact, right now I prefer it," she said and went to take a sip from her glass, when the others joined them.

"No kiss hello?" Logic asked, and pressed close and kissed her cheek. She looked at him, that sexy crew cut hair, and sultry smile. Her heart raced. She then leaned into Train, who kissed her on the mouth, surprising her.

She pulled back. "Train, don't," she said, only for Brew to pull her close. He cupped her neck and head under her hair and wrapped her up tight in his muscular arms.

"We have a lot to talk about, and I expect answers and the truth," he said and kissed her. When he released her lips she exhaled in annoyance.

"That's not how this works," she told him.

"Well, we either talk or I throw you over my shoulder, we head out of here right now and I take you home to talk," he said very seriously.

"It isn't that simple, Brew."

"You don't need to tell me. None of this is simple, baby. It's fucking complicated, messy, and for some fucking insane reason, you, I want more of it. I want you. We all do. Let's talk and listen, something we failed to do the other morning at your place," he said and tears filled her eyes. Royce hugged her from behind.

"Just a conversation, and then we see where it goes."

She looked at Royce and Brew then Logic, and Train.

"I saw you when you came in. How the women flocked to you, calling you by name. I don't want that. I don't want to be…I won't be just another woman you had in your bed."

Royce narrowed his eyes at her. "First, no other women have shared our bed in our penthouse, ever, and we have never shared the same woman before. We know the difference between you and women like that," he said to her.

"I'm not so sure you do," she said and then turned away from them and toward the bar.

"Being vulnerable is an emotion none of us are comfortable with," Logic said to her. She glanced at him.

"Just as jealousy can make a person do stupid things, like maybe stray toward another," Train added.

"You strayed?" she asked, feeling insulted, jealous, hurt.

"Not us, you," Brew said to her.

"Me? I didn't stray," she said, pointing at her chest.

"The two dicks in the newspaper. That pompous asshole Antonio and the other dick," Brew added.

"That's business," she said and went to turn, only for Brew to grip her tight and crush her between the bar and himself. She held his gaze, her head tilted up toward his face.

"You let them touch you. Did you let them kiss you, pleasure you?" he hissed at her. She shook her head. He looked and sounded so fierce but also hurt.

She felt his hand cup her ass and squeeze. "Brew."

"This is our body. You're our woman. We fucked up and we know that. This is new, Alda, and we aren't going to be a bunch of fucking pussies and pour our emotions out to you or snuggle on the couch and talk about secrets or things that make us who we are. We just aren't those types of men," he said to her. Tears filled her eyes.

"I just expected something, Brew. Anything you would give me, a morsel of something personal about each of you. I was willing to accept your denial of your feelings. I know what type of men you are, but I didn't expect to be diverted, then told how busy of a week it would be and that you all weren't sure when we could get together, and then you ask for my key to my apartment. You didn't even take me out on a date? Is that not acceptable either? Does that fall under making you all feel vulnerable?" she asked and a tear fell. She wiped it away and pushed against his arms.

"No. You're right. We should have been honest, but if we were, then you would have known how weak you make us," Brew said to her. She couldn't believe it. Brew of all of them was the hardest, the most demanding and rough.

"He speaks the truth, Alda. We're sorry we hurt you. That we made you feel unimportant to us. It's the last thing we wanted to do," Royce said to her.

"Letting those men touch you, kiss you or more, won't go unpunished though either," Train said to her. Her eyes widened and Brew chuckled then pulled her close again, his hand squeezed her ass.

"First things first," Brew said, holding her gaze then lowering down to kiss her. When his lips touched hers, none of what happened yesterday morning even mattered, nor the crazy thoughts that bothered her all day. All that mattered was being surrounded by these four men, kissed and taken by them. Everything else was minimal.

* * * *

Alda was sitting on Brew's lap in one of the chairs at a long table and the men were gathered around her, touching her, caressing her skin and talking to her about things being so different. Once they got through the awkwardness of explaining their childhoods and being adopted, she really seemed to relax and let down that guard she had up most of the night. Royce still wondered what she did with Antonio and his cousin, but she apologized for sort of cheating on them and kissing other men. They caused her to do it, so he had to forgive her, but the jealous feeling ate him up inside, and he knew he was never going to let Alda out of his sight.

"So why this sexy dress tonight? Were you planning on making us drool?" Logic asked and eased his palm up and down her thigh then over her knee.

"I had backup plans," she said and then looked away from them.

"Back up plans?" Brew asked.

She turned in his arms. Royce saw her cheeks blush.

"I didn't know how things would turn out here and I had a plan B," she told them.

"Did plan B involve other men?" Royce asked.

"Well, it involved a cocktail party in a penthouse in Times Square," she said and then stood up and fixed her dress. Brew grabbed her hand and Train stood up behind her.

"Those two dicks live in a penthouse in Times Square?" Brew asked.

"No, a friend of theirs was throwing a party and I was invited. I told them I may not make it. Plan B," she said.

Train gripped her shoulders and massaged them as he whispered into her ear but they could all hear.

"Brew and the rest of us had a plan B too in case you didn't fully cooperate," Train told her.

"Guys," Royce said but it was too late as Brew bent and pulled her up over his shoulder. He kept a hand on her ass as she screamed and yelled at him to put her down.

"Good night, all," Brew yelled to their friends, who all hooted and hollered, laughing and cheering them on as Brew and Train walked out of the room and through the crowd with Alda over Brew's shoulder. Logic looked at Royce and shook his head.

"Plan B wasn't necessary. She was cooperating and listening."

"I think Brew and Train just want her alone, and naked, pretty much as we do." Logic laughed as they followed their brothers out of the club.

"I also think Brew and Train wanted everyone to see us all leave with Alda and with her over his shoulder. Maybe it's his way of saying we're off the market and so is Alda," Royce said and Logic slapped his brother's shoulder and smiled wide. Nothing was going to get in the way of making Alda all theirs. Nothing.

* * * *

Alda gasped when Brew set her feet down on the ground by the SUV and then turned her around and smacked her ass. "Get in," he demanded.

"What?" she replied as she went to move, but apparently not fast enough as Brew scooped her up again into his arms, this time in a cradle position and slid into the back seat. Train followed and Royce and Logic got in up front. She was embarrassed, shaking, aroused, annoyed, turned on, and then moaning as Brew pressed his lips to hers and kissed her again. When he pulled from her lips, she reprimanded him. "How could you do that to me, Brew? All those people watching and whistling, yelling as you acted like a bunch of cavemen," she said. He looked so serious as he held her gaze and then licked his lips.

"I had enough of the talking. That's how you make me feel, baby. Wild, animalistic, desperate to claim your body, mark you, make everyone know who you belong to and then make love to you and pound it into you, so you never stray again. It's barbaric, I fucking know it, but that's what you do to all of us. I can't explain in words. I know that somehow pissed you off before and made you stray but not again. You accept my actions. Our actions and understand them, damn it," he told her then kissed her again. She was turned on by his words, his desperate need that mimicked hers.

Train ran his hand up her thigh and she parted them for him. He scooted closer.

"Don't push us away. We don't know what the fuck we're doing. We've never been serious about a woman, had a girlfriend, never mind one we all want, shared and continue to want you," Train told her.

Brew pulled from her lips and she looked at Train, her lips parted, her breathing hitched. "I don't want to feel used," she whispered, tears falling from her eyes.

"Never. We're sorry if we made you feel that way. Maybe we need to do more feeling, more touching, and zone in on the power and connection we all have?"

He stroked her thigh and gripped the upper part then slid his hand down again. It felt so good, so right. Then Brew cupped her breast, caressed a thumb over the nipple, arousing her further. Her legs parted, accepting Train's exploration. That desperate need built up inside of her.

"That's right. You know when one of us touches you that you're to obey our commands and give us what we desire," Train said to her and stroked along her groin. Her lips parted and Brew helped Train push the material of her dress to her hips. "Red fucking panties. She's wearing tiny red lace panties," Train said.

"For us, not for those fucktards!" Logic yelled from the front seat, shocking her. He seemed so calm, and less aggressive than the others.

The SUV slowed down.

"Come here," Train ordered. Brew eased her up off his lap and Train lifted her like she weighed hardly anything at all onto his lap. He cupped her cheeks and hair, held her gaze and looked over her lips. "You belong to us. You need to accept what that means in every way. Do you understand me, Alda? In every way, you give full control over you to us. There's no other way to make this relationship work. No wasting time on worrying about things that don't exist, you'll know you belong to us only and there will be no other men and no other women. Understand and accept?"

She stared at him, her heart racing, her pussy throbbing with need. Even her ass tingled in anticipation, and enjoyment of what it felt like when they all made love together.

"Yes, Train. I want that." He pressed his lips to hers gently and when he pulled back the SUV stopped.

"When we get you upstairs, you slowly undress for us, and then you are to place your hands on the edge of the bed, legs spread wide, ass lifted, and you accept your punishment from us."

She gasped.

"What? What do you mean, punishment?" she asked and wondered why she felt aroused, intrigued by this dominance and control they demanded over her.

Brew stroked her jaw as the door opened.

"For letting two other men touch you, kiss you, press you between them and want you, when you belong to the four of us." He tapped her jaw.

"Now move," Train stated.

She looked to the left and there stood Royce. Logic was right behind him, arms crossed and a fierce expression on his face.

Train lifted her off his lap to Royce. Royce helped her out and she fixed her dress. She noticed that Logic held her purse and the phone was out of it and with the purse. Before she could ask him anything Royce pulled her against him, wrapped his arms around her waist and kissed her. She felt his palm grab her ass then lift her thigh up against his hip as he plunged his tongue into her mouth. That kiss was hot, filled with desire and so commanding she relaxed in his arms until he released her lips and then gave her body a little shake.

"You are in for it tonight." He gave her ass a smack as he set her straight and then turned her to walk toward the elevator in the underground parking garage. Logic turned away and stepped in first. They all followed. He didn't look at her but passed her phone to Train and then to Brew. Royce's hand tightened on hers. She looked up at him and he was staring straight ahead and appeared as if he were biting the inside of his cheek. Was he still angry with her? Were they really going to punish her, spank her ass, and expect her to obey their order?

She gulped as the doors opened and then they walked down the small hall to another elevator, stepped inside and then Logic punched in the code and the doors closed and then opened a few seconds later to the other hallway before their penthouse. As they got inside Royce released her hand.

"To the bedroom and do as you were told," he said to her. All four men stared at her, looking serious and stern. Train rotated her cell phone in his hand.

"Train, what are you doing with my phone?" she asked.

"It was going off on our way here."

She swallowed hard. It didn't take a genius to tell that whomever texted her said something that upset them.

"Who was it and what did they say, since apparently you read it?" she asked all of them.

They were quiet.

"All control of you, Alda. It's what we require and need stepping forward. It's the kind of men we are, our professions and the way we need this relationship to be," Royce said to her, mimicking Train and Brew's words to her earlier.

"I understand," she said and waited, thought about this. The text was probably from Antonio. He expected to see her tonight. He hinted about spending time alone with him, but she realized she was being stupid and looking for excuses to stay clear of Brew, Royce, Train, and Logic out of fear of the uncertainty, but their actions since they arrived at the club showed her how upset they were, too. How they missed her, hadn't meant to make her feel like used goods, but that they had commitment issues, never had a girlfriend but were making an effort their way. She could accept that because she cared about them, hell, maybe even fell in love somewhere between their stupidity and hers.

She reached back and undid the zipper on her dress slowly. "It doesn't matter what he said. What any man other than the four of you says or wants. I don't belong to him. I've never belonged to any man, and as much as it scares me to tell you I belong to each of you, it arouses me. Makes me wet, and only the four of you get that reaction." She let the dress fall, saw their hunger in their eyes and she stepped from the dress, then reached back and unclipped her bra.

"Forget the texts. I'll be in the bedroom, in position as ordered," she said, dropped the bra, let them get an eyeful of her and she walked down the hallway as sexy as possible with her legs shaking, her heart racing and wondering whether the ass spanking would hurt, or make her fall deeper under their spell.

As she entered their bedroom, Royce's from what she remembered them saying, she stepped from her heels and the thong panties and then got herself into the position they told her to. Every inch of her was oversensitive, even her palms as they hit the thick, white comforter. Her forearms tingled, then her shoulders, her pussy, ass, and thighs as she sensed them entering the room. They were quiet, but their presence a force field of masculinity, toughness and macho-ness she just couldn't describe fully, or its effect on every one of her body parts.

As a palm glided along her ass, she hissed and tightened.

"You think that little speech will make us go easy on you? Think again," Royce stated firmly.

She looked to the right, Brew was naked already.

"Eyes closed," Logic ordered, cupping her chin, making her turn to the left.

She saw him naked, his thick long cock dripping already with pre-cum. She licked her lips.

"Closed," Train ordered from behind her with Royce.

She closed her eyes and gripped the comforter. Hands encased her wrists on both sides by Train and Brew.

"Relax. Everything we do to you, to this body, is for your pleasure and ours. You accepted our dominance and control. Now relax and receive your punishment," Train told her as he and Brew caressed up and down her forearms then gripped her wrists just as the first smack landed on her ass cheek.

"Oh," she gasped, not expecting the combined sensation of being restrained and the hand on her ass. She jerked and then the second hand smacked her ass. Her pussy throbbed and leaked.

"Those men can't have you. You're ours," Logic said and then smacked her ass hard.

"Oh God. Oh." She moaned and her pussy leaked.

Smack, smack.

"Ours," Royce commanded.

"Yes. Oh God, yes, I am. I want that. Please," she begged.

"Ours," Brew said to her and kissed the top of her head.

"Always," Train said and kissed her head. They both eased their large, firm hands up her arms to her shoulders.

Smack, smack. She jerked forward and Train and Brew stepped back and Logic and Royce took their places. Logic gripped a fistful of her hair and lifted her head toward him. She opened her eyes. "I need so badly it burns in my heart. It actually burns. It's foreign for me, Alda," he said to her, his eyes so serious and emotional.

She blinked. "I feel it, too." *Smack. Smack.* Her lips parted, her voice cracked.

"Yours. Make me all yours," she said and Logic lowered down and kissed her. When he lifted up he climbed onto the bed and brought his cock to her lips just as fingers slid into her cunt.

Her gasp was stopped by the thick bulbous top of Logic's cock. She sucked and moaned.

Smack, smack, smack.

She tightened and came.

"Fuck," Brew roared. She bobbed her head up and down as Brew removed his fingers and replaced them with his cock. He shoved right into her from behind, his fingers dug into her hips and he rocked deeply. Her breasts bounced and swayed as Royce cupped one and Train caressed her back. They were all touching her, taking from her, possessing her.

"Heaven. Your body is heaven and I'll never get enough, Alda. Never," Brew stated and rocked faster and faster.

Logic's hands gripped her hair tighter. "Fuck, her mouth is perfection," Logic said.

"Train, the lube. We need her together," Royce stated.

Brew pulled out, she moaned but then Logic pulled from her mouth.

"Logic," she called out and moved toward him to take his cock back into her mouth but the men had other plans. Train slid in underneath her as Brew lifted her up and placed her onto his cock. She lowered down and took him inside of her as she ran her palms up and down his chest, gripping his muscles, needing to absorb the feel of him. Then Logic gripped her hair again and brought her mouth to his cock. "Together, as one, the way we'll always be," he said and she held his gaze as she accepted his cock in her mouth while Train thrust up into her cunt.

Fingers filled with lube pushed into her ass and it burned at first before the need, the desire overtook all else. In and out Brew thrust lubed fingers into her ass and then cursed.

"Fuck, I'm going to come just from watching her asshole suck in my fingers."

Smack, smack.

She jerked, not expecting the smacks to her ass. Then Brew's fingers pulled out and his cock replaced them.

"Ours. We own every inch of this body, your heart and your soul, just as you own ours," Brew said fiercely then slid into her ass. They all moaned and the thrusting, chanting, lovemaking began at once.

In and out, up and down they worked together to satisfy their needs. Logic came, shooting his seed down her throat and then Brew came next, grunting and rocking. *Smack, smack, smack.* He spanked her hard and she cried out another release.

"I love fucking and spanking this ass. This body is exceptional and made for us," Brew said and slid out of her ass. Royce took his place, sliding his palms along her body, gripping her hair and kissing her on the mouth before trailing his mouth along her shoulder, her spine as Train thrust his hips harder, faster, upward. She gasped, losing her breath from Train's strokes and then cried out, her voice cracking as Royce thrust into her ass. The two men worked their cocks deeper, ran their hands everywhere, cupping her breasts, tweaking the nipples and then moaning and growling like cavemen. "Ours. She's ours, brothers," Royce yelled out.

"Fuck yeah," Train said and came. Royce continued to thrust into her then growled out loudly. "Alda!" he exclaimed and came inside of her.

Alda collapsed to Train's chest and he cuddled her, caressed her skin. When Royce pulled from her ass and caressed it she moaned at the tenderness. Brew chuckled.

"A nice pink ass. Remember that next time some other man approaches wanting a kiss to the cheek, a harmless hug. We see that and all hell will break loose on that ass," Brew said and spanked it.

"Brew!" she reprimanded. His words so carnal and wild. Train chuckled, the rumbling in his chest against her ear made her insides giddy. She couldn't believe what just took place. She allowed four men to spank her ass, punish her as they called it and claim ownership of her body, heart and soul. She should be mortified, embarrassed, and…hell no, she felt amazing, cherished and loved. She wanted to be their possession, if that was what being the lover, girlfriend of made men meant. She would learn to understand their words, their actions as examples of their desire and care for her. She realized how much she cared for them and when she thought about work, about Antonio, Tatum and her career, they meant nothing without having these men as hers.

She lifted up as Train pulled from her body and eased her to the side. Brew and Logic were there to clean her up with washcloth and towel. She reached up and cupped Logic's cheek.

"I don't care about work, about what they think or that I won't be able to be the cover model for the cosmetic line. I care about the four of you more. I can find another job. I'm not scared. I have money saved and—"

"Whoa, whoa, what are you talking about?" Brew asked, cupping her cheek.

She lowered her hand from his and Train finished wiping off his cock with the towel and turned toward her. "They said something to you about us?" Train asked.

"Haley was saying that it would look terrible if the public found out that I was screwing four men, that it would be bad for the company," she told them. Brew narrowed his eyes at her and Train cupped her cheek.

"Sorry she said that to you. A lot of people don't understand this type of relationship," Train said to her.

"It's new to all of us, baby, but we wouldn't do anything to jeopardize your job, or your happiness. If this means that much to you to do this cover model thing—" Logic added to the conversation and she interrupted him.

"No, no, Logic, being with the four of you means everything to me. I actually felt pretty uncomfortable doing the shoots, and posing for the product line. I don't really want to do it if it means being away from the four of you."

"You would need to travel and do gigs and stuff?" Royce asked, joining them on the bed.

"There was that possibility, but ultimately it's really just my face, my body that's a representative for the makeup line," she told them. Train caressed her cheek.

"You're a gorgeous, sexy woman, they would be crazy not to use you because of your personal lifestyle."

"I know that, and you know that, but Haley, Antonio, and his company have the final say. I've worked so hard bringing MAX

Industries and their products to the public eye. Maxwell, my boss, who is super nice, is so proud of me and thankful," she told him.

"What does he say about all of this?" Brew asked her.

She thought about that a moment.

"I don't know. I haven't spoken to him really. He kind of put a lot of the control in Haley's hands. She's the one that knows Antonio and Tatum so well."

"I don't like her at all. There is just something about her, about that Antonio guy too that's off," Royce stated.

She looked at him. "What do you mean?" she asked.

He explained their feelings and observations, and how Antonio hadn't really reacted seeing their guns or maybe knowing they were made men. She thought about that, too.

"He's pretty pompous and confident," she replied.

"Got that from the text messages alone," Logic stated, looking angry again. He reached out and stroked her breast. She held his gaze.

"What did he say?" she asked.

"Doesn't matter. Hopefully your lack of response will be enough," Logic said. She lifted up. Logic stood up by the edge of the bed and she knelt on her knees and reached out to him.

"Don't be jealous, Logic. I'm here with you, aren't I?" she asked him. He stroked her hair and she caressed his muscles on his chest. He ran his palms along her back and to her ass then back to her cheeks. He cupped them.

"Yes, you are here with all of us. That's why I'm not raging still. However, it is going to take a lot more love making to really ease this jealous, angry feeling inside of me."

She lifted up and kissed his chin.

"I'm yours. I accept all of your rules, your commands, your possession of my body, heart and soul. Are all of you mine, too, body heart and soul, because it's all or nothing, Logic, Brew, Train, and Royce," she said and turned to look at each of them.

"Oh baby, you did not just threaten us," Royce said, looking at her sideways. She licked her lips and stared at his cock as it grew before her eyes.

"What if I did?" she teased.

Smack. Train spanked her ass.

"Round two begins now. I don't think she got the message," Brew said and Logic released her hips as Brew wrapped an arm around her waist, hoisted her back to the bed and then pressed over her body, spreading her thighs wide with her arms pressed above her head.

"You've got a lot to learn about being the woman of made men," he said to her and held her gaze.

"Teach me," she stated.

"Oh man, she is asking for it," Train said, rolling over to cup her breast.

"And she is going to get it," Brew told her and kissed her lips, then her breasts, down her belly to her cunt.

"Oh, Brew." She moaned.

"You have a lot to learn, Alda, and we are definitely the men to teach you," Royce said and all of them began to kiss her, arouse her and get her ready to take them all inside of her again. She loved them, and it didn't scare her to admit that, it made her accept them and their dominant, controlling ways even more, and nothing else mattered but loving them all.

Chapter 11

"I think we have a problem," Salento said to Lou Carvetti.

"What problem would that be?" Lou asked.

"The guys you have picking up the shit and doing the deliveries, they're skimming off the top. They're also selling on Garlitto territory. I can't have any fuck ups, man. No one can know that we're involved with this drug."

"I can take care of it. Have them move elsewhere just as a precaution. I'm sure Garlitto knows nothing," Lou stated.

"That won't be for long. Some dicks gave the pill to a friend of the Coglonies, Fiorres and fucking Royce Brooks and his psycho team of guys. They're after blood because they knew the woman as well as another woman that could have been drugged."

"Holy fuck. Of all the fucking bitches to try and snag, some assholes chooses them, women associated with the families. Shit."

"Exactly. If they find out we're connected, those men will think nothing of offing us."

"What do you want to do, Salento? We can pull back now."

"They're asking a lot of questions. You need to call in the guys and make sure they know to seal their fucking lips."

"Who were the two women?" Lou asked.

"The fuck if I know. Why?"

"Just asking to see if I know who they are. All those men hang out with hot fucking women. Classy, professional ones, not whores."

"My guy, the one making this stuff, has his eyes set on some woman. He was pretty fucking pissed that she didn't show up at the party last night. He isn't planning on staying in New York much longer. His cousin is a fucking psycho though. Something is wrong with that guy. Anyway, just secure the guys you have and make sure they keep their fucking mouths shut."

"Got it. By the way, we sold out fast. This whole waiting for supply thing is genius. People are willing to pay whatever price we put on the pills."

"Well, keep it at a thousand for now. I'm hoping to get another supply in shortly. Like I said, he hinted about leaving town for a bit. Take care of things. I'll be in touch."

* * * *

C.J. Ruffinno looked at the picture in the newspaper his mom showed him. She was so proud of Alda and her accomplishments. News of the potential opportunity as cover model for a makeup line at the company she worked for was in negotiations. What he hadn't expected to see was the picture with her and two men. The one man was the one who handed over the large bag of drugs to him and Fogerty the other night. How was this guy connected? He needed to ask Fogerty about him. Did his cousin know what this guy was into? C.J. had the feeling that this was coincidence. Fogerty carried on about no one knowing who the guy was that supplied the drugs but that he was wealthy, had connections overseas and was into crazy shit. Could one of these men, or both, be the main supplier?

His phone buzzed and he saw it was Fogerty.

Meet me in twenty minutes at the Station House bar. It's urgent.

He didn't like the sound of that as he stood up from the table and downed the rest of the iced tea.

"Mom, I need to go. Thanks for lunch."

"Sure, honey. Isn't that great news about Alda? Her parents would be so proud if they were alive. She's really turned into something special. So independent and professional."

"I know, she's a knockout, too. I'm sure she'll get that position if it's what she wants."

"Oh, she will, I'm sure, although she doesn't like the spotlight," his mom said and looked at the picture again.

"Such handsome men. Do you think she's dating them?" she asked. Surprised that her mom included both men, he squinted at her.

"Honey, she hangs out with a lot of friends in ménage relationships. I wouldn't be surprised at all. In fact, I'm shocked none of those men have gone after Alda for themselves. She's a catch."

"I haven't heard anything, and I don't know about the two men in the picture. Next time I see her at one of the clubs I'll ask."

"Okay. Take care."

"Bye," he said and kissed her good-bye then headed out. Twenty minutes later he walked into the Station House Bar.

"Got a call from Carvetti. There's been some concern over some of the connected families trying to find out who is supplying the drugs and dealing them. Apparently there was a situation a week or so ago at one of the clubs and some guy used the drug on two women. One drank the drink and he attempted to force her out of the club but was stopped."

"Oh shit. What do you know?"

"Well, that's where this gets crazy. You especially need to keep your fucking mouth shut." C.J. swallowed.

"It was Alessa the guy drugged and apparently your cousin Alda had it in her drink but didn't drink it. She was the one to stop the guy from leaving. It turned into a mess of a situation."

"What? Was Alda hurt and Alessa?" he asked.

"No, calm down. If they were, would I fucking be here telling you? No, it was no big deal. Your cousin didn't drink the shit. Alessa did but Cobra and his friends took care of her," Fogerty whispered.

"Holy shit. Of all the women to use this shit on. Jesus, I don't know, Fogerty. This is too fucking close to home. Like I said the other night on that delivery, I don't want to be involved with this."

"It's too late for that. I need you. I chose you out of everyone else to help me do these deals and get a huge cut."

"You also are pushing your luck with Garlitto."

"That's resolved. We're moving our location. The bosses need to set something up out of town anyway. If this operation is to move forward, and we keep doing the deals smoothly with no bumps then we're in. We get to maintain our position and make more money and get a bigger cut. That means no more shit jobs. We'll be working for Carvetti and Salento."

"Salento Sorenno? That's the dealer?" he asked.

"He's the middleman working for the guy who is dealing the drugs."

"Who is the dealer then?"

"I don't know and I don't care. Asking questions isn't smart. What I did hear is that the guy has his eyes on some woman and is going out of town, probably with her for a period of time."

C.J. felt his gut clench. Who was the woman? Was the guy in the picture with Alda, the one he met the other night, the guy dealing the drugs? Did Alda know? He needed to find out. What if his cousin didn't know the guy was into that shit, or what if he used it on her? Fuck.

"What's wrong?"

"The guy we met and got the drugs from the other night, is he the dealer?"

"Didn't I just say asking questions wasn't smart?"

"Fogerty, I have my reasons. Is he or not?"

"What fucking reasons do you have other than curiosity that can get us both killed?"

"Just answer me. If I'm going to be in on this shit and making money I want to know who to watch and look out for."

"Fine, I don't know who he is. I assume he's a main connection to the guy because Carvetti and Solento are the only two other people that know any of this. It can't be more than the five of us. I'm pretty sure the guy we met is the one taking the calls for the orders, so he must work side by side with the boss."

C.J. ran his fingers through his hair and exhaled.

"What is it?"

"Nothing."

"Bullshit, nothing, what the fuck is it?"

"I was at my mom's house this morning and she showed me the paper. Alda was in a picture posing between two big shot businessmen investing in the company she works for. Alda may be the cover image for the cosmetic line."

Fogerty whistled. "Dude, your cousin is super fucking hot. Like hard on as soon as a man puts his eyes on her."

"You really?" C.J. yelled at him and Fogerty raised his hands up.

"Just stating the fucking obvious. You think she's fucking the two guys? I mean, what's with the concern?" Fogerty asked.

He stared at him, debating about telling him.

"One of the guys in the picture, he's the one we got the shit from the other night."

Fogerty's eyes widened and he sat forward. He didn't say a word and then he whistled again.

"Holy shit, your cousin is dating him?"

"I don't know. I just saw the picture of them together and between both men. We don't know who the main boss is, but what if it's the two men?"

"Then your cousin is set for fucking life. These guys make mad money and would surely want only the best women around them. Your cousin is hot, professional and if she's the cover model for makeup products then of course the guys would want a woman like that on their arms."

"What if she doesn't know?"

"Who cares? They have to keep an image, maybe a cover to protect their real lives. As long as your cousin is safe then it's all good." He gave C.J. a slap to his arm.

"It also puts us at an even higher advantage. Once he finds out you're related, he'll probably give us better positions in the business and we'll be making a shit load of money and have our own beauties on our arms like your cousin in no time."

C.J. stared at him, his concern was for his cousin.

"Dude, stop worrying about who your cousin is fucking. She hangs out with made men all the fucking time. Her friends are doing a bunch of them. She can take care of herself, obviously. Now remember, you have to keep your mouth shut. No one can know what we know or we'll get whacked. This is heavy shit. So get that look off your face and focus. She's a grown woman and if she spreads her legs then she needs to handle the consequences of who she does that for. Although knowing Alda, she's making those men work for it. She isn't easy. Not by a long shot."

"She probably doesn't have a clue that they're dealing drugs then."

"Not your problem right now, besides, like I said, the main guy is leaving town for a few days. Let's make the changes and be ready for the next shipment and sale. Okay?"

"Okay, but if I catch wind of anything that puts Alda in serious danger, I'm telling her."

"Hey, that's your suicide, not mine. My lips are sealed. I'm in this to make more money. What we made so far is peanuts compared to what we will make as this grows. Think like a boss, not like a sissy."

* * * *

Royce held her against his body, his palm over her ass as she hugged him good-bye. She leaned up and kissed his chin and he smiled at her.

"Do you have to go in for this meeting?" he asked.

"You know I do. We spent all day Sunday in bed, and I called in sick Monday. I have to go back to work," she said to him. She eased back and so did he but kept his arms around her waist.

"What are you going to do about Antonio and Tatum?" Brew asked her.

She smiled at him, reached out and took his hand, brought it to her lips and kissed his knuckles. His mean expression softened. "I won't be alone with them, Brew. The most that will happen is a lunch meeting or something with them and Haley and Maxwell. I think I'm going to tell them I changed my mind about the modeling."

Royce squeezed her hips. "Wait, don't do that because you think that's what we want."

She pressed her hand to his chest.

"I'm not. I thought about it," she said and looked at him, then Brew, Train, and Logic who all stood in her kitchen. They had driven her home early this morning so she could shower and dress for work.

"I don't want to be apart from you guys. I also don't want anyone questioning my judgment, my personal life and who I care about. If it means losing my job, then so be it. If Maxwell lets me go over this then he isn't the man I thought he was."

"Hopefully it won't come to that," Brew said to her. She smiled.

"Well, you guys need to head to work and so do I."

Royce released her to Brew so she could kiss him good-bye and then to Logic and Train. Train caressed her ass, then ran his thumb along her lower lip and clenched her chin.

"Do you need to wear something so sexy as this?" he asked.

She slid to the side and smoothed the material of the dress back into place.

"It's business attire," she countered.

Brew stroked a finger along her neck and the V of the top that exposed some of her cleavage as well as a designer necklace.

"This is a lot of skin," Brew stated. She placed her hand on his hip.

"I'm yours though, remember."

He pulled her close. "I remember, and I hope you do, too. Perhaps tonight you'll need some more training," he teased and pressed his lips to hers.

She pulled back. "You are making it so difficult to leave right now."

"Good," all four men said at the same time, making her blush, her belly quiver and giddiness fill her heart. She smiled.

Oh yeah, I'm in love with them. Won't tell them yet. That could send them over the edge.

She smiled as they headed out of her apartment, together.

* * * *

"She slept with them. Spent the fucking weekend in their arms, not ours." Tatum raised his voice. Antonio had his hands on his hips and a scowl on his face.

"I'm as angry as you are and didn't see this coming. I should have known when she didn't show up at the party and didn't acknowledge my texts. I should have picked her up and made her come before she had a chance to go to the club and let those four men seduce her into bed. I fucked up."

"Well, you need to make this up to me. I want her. She fits in every way. You and I both know this."

"Calm down and stop thinking about fucking her."

"I'm thinking about more than that. The whole fantasy, Antonio. Don't tell me you haven't imagined it, too."

"Of course I have and especially since the other night when we both kissed her and held her between us."

"Then we need a plan. Maybe we should head out tonight. I think the longer we wait the harder it will be to get her to accept us," Tatum said to Antonio.

"We have the upper hand, Tatum. If she doesn't leave willingly then we do what is necessary." Tatum nodded.

* * * *

"A lot is riding on this, Alda. You can't blow off Antonio and Tatum for some wild fling with four men who won't take you seriously. Your job is riding on this. It needs to be resolved before they leave for a business trip upstate," Haley told her.

"I don't appreciate you coming here and putting this pressure on me. My personal life is none of your business. I don't know why so much is riding on whether or not I get romantically involved with Antonio and Tatum. That isn't going to happen. I'm in a relationship with someone else."

"Are you serious? You're choosing a relationship with them over one with Tatum and Antonio? Men who care about you, will take you seriously, support you, and commit to you?"

"Excuse me, but you do not know the men I'm involved with. They are committed to me and I am committed to them. Now, this conversation is over. Now do you have something to discuss with me business wise or not?" She raised her voice at Haley, who looked shocked. Alda didn't really care. She realized in that moment that this job didn't mean as much to her even though she put so much effort into building the company and the products. Was it because she had a safety net, her four lovers who promised to take care of her and provide for her? Not that she would let them. She was an independent woman but it did give her peace of mind and a bit of confidence while facing Haley. The woman was a feared boss in the company.

Haley narrowed her eyes at her. Then she pointed at her.

"You better not screw up this deal with Antonio. His company can provide the best arrangements for us here and for Maxwell. In fact, we'll see how Maxwell feels about this situation and whether you have a job here anymore."

Haley walked out of the office and slammed the door closed.

Alda leaned back in her chair and exhaled. She felt nervous, unsure, but went about doing her job. She texted Royce and told him what happened and about Antonio and Tatum leaving for upstate for business and it was probably a good thing. He gave her supportive words, and made her feel better and then she told him she couldn't wait to see them tonight after work.

We'll have a double pomegranate martini waiting for you, honey, he texted back and she smiled wide and chuckled. Her four men had instantly become her rocks, her everything.

* * * *

"What do you want me to do? Maxwell isn't here today. Everyone is busy finalizing things. It looks like your personal plans are falling through," Haley said to him.

"Not falling through, just altered slightly," Antonio told her and looked at Tatum, who stared out the window.

"Call her for a meeting in an hour, at the back meeting room. Say we're going over importing and exporting details as well as appearances for her to do as the cover model for the project."

"You're keeping her in that position anyway?" Haley asked.

"We made some changes this morning. Our other deal is taking a change of direction and this whole idea of overseas sales can wait a bit. No rush, and it will give us time to convince Alda who she really belongs to," Antonio told her.

Haley exhaled. "So you still want her, despite who she's been with."

"That isn't your concern."

"I've been here for you. I helped to set this whole thing up with Maxwell so you can do your thing and I can get my cut. Now you want to hold off so you can fuck some whore."

Before Antonio could react, Tatum was across the room and gripping Haley by the neck. She gasped and grabbed onto his wrists.

"You don't ever talk about her or say anything negative. She is better than you, that's why you're jealous. Watch what you say and do, Haley, or you'll wind up dead," Tatum said then shoved her away. Antonio squinted at her as she coughed and backed up.

"Get it together. Get her here for a meeting and we'll take care of the rest," Antonio told her.

She hurried out of the room and Tatum stared at the door as it closed. One look at that expression, those eyes and he knew that Tatum was close to losing it. "Patience, Tatum. We need to play this very carefully and strike when she least expects it."

"I know, Antonio. I know, but Haley pisses me off. She set me up. She gave me those drugs and I nearly killed that woman."

Antonio swallowed. That woman died by his cousin's hands but his cousin didn't know it.

"That's over and we know not to trust her."

"Then she should be taken care of, too."

"Leaving bodies around is not smart business. Let's stay focused on what we want. Isn't that why we created the drug, and put it out there? To bring something unique and profitable in the game of life."

"How long will we have to run the business hands on?"

"Not long. Salento will be our bitch in this. A seventy/thirty cut of everything. Seventy for us, and we control the amount distributed. We can focus on our life with our desires and wants and no interference. We have more than enough money and a continuous cash flow coming in. Relax. It will work out fine, and Alda will be right there with us along the way."

Chapter 12

Alda didn't want to go to this meeting. She was so nervous. She felt uncomfortable seeing Antonio and Tatum, knowing they liked her and that they knew she slept with Royce, Brew, Logic, and Train, and committed to them. She was basically choosing the four men over the two of them.

When she arrived at the meeting room, the smaller one at the back of the building by the stairs, she got an eerie feeling. Probably because it would be only her, Tatum, Antonio, and Haley in the room. As she entered they greeted her with smiles and her gut clenched.

"So glad you're feeling better and were able to come in to work today," Antonio said to her, smiling and looking her over. Suddenly she thought about Brew's words of concern over her dress. Perhaps it did show off a bit more skin than necessary. She did love the dress. No, she was being silly because of the situation.

"Thank you, I'm feeling great. So what's this all about?" she asked as Tatum held out a chair for her. Each of the seats had a folder and a bottle of water in front of it.

"Let me get that for you," Tatum said to Haley, unscrewing the cap on her bottle. Alda reached for hers and Antonio offered the same thing.

"Let me get that while you look at the folder and the picture we thought was perfect to place on the main cartons of makeup," he said and took her water bottle, opened it while she looked at the folder. When she opened it up she was shocked at the image. It was perfect. Not too large but definitely a symbol of a cover image associated with all the products. She placed her hand over her belly and had a mix of emotions. She felt excited about the images and product and being chosen, but also a bit nervous to take it on and especially if her personal life was an issue.

"I know it's a lot to take in, but no one can deny how perfect you fit on there, Alda," Haley said to her.

"It's amazing. I can't believe I'm on the cover of a product like this," she said then reached for the water bottle and took a long sip. She placed it down but remained holding it.

"I know things have changed. Business is business though, and we'd be foolish to remove you just because we're disappointed by personal choices in your life," Antonio said to her.

"Not smart choices," Tatum added and she squinted at him. Antonio cleared his throat.

"He's still feeling jealous and disappointed. Aside from that, in the file you'll see that we've gone and crunched numbers, talked about aspects we can use to properly ship and export the packages, but first there's the concern over the size of each one. You see here, the multipack is bulky, we don't want to take away from your image or the product image. What do you think?" he asked her and she looked at the photos. She had to blink a few times, as her vision blurred and then sharpened. She felt a little lightheaded and went to take a bit more water. She finished the bottle and then Antonio reached over and caressed her cheek with the back of his hand.

"Are you feeling okay, Alda? You look a little pale," he said to her.

She leaned back. "I, I don't know why. I was fine, before." She heard her slurred speech and felt it.

"Now, Antonio?" Tatum asked.

"I'll look to make sure it's all clear," Haley said and Alda felt confused. She reached for her cell phone in her bag and laid her head on the table. She didn't know what numbers she pushed and then she dropped it. The chair pulled back.

"I'll carry her, you get the car ready so we can get her to the house. Haley, cover everything up."

"Oh shit," Haley said.

Alda grabbed on to her arm. "Help me. Please, I don't feel right. I feel dizzy," she said loudly.

"Move it now. Fuck," Tatum yelled and Alda felt her body bouncing but it was like slow motion. Then the blood rushed to her head and she felt it swish side to side, hitting her ears, her eyes and then her mouth.

"Antonio, please."

"I've got you, baby. We're going to take good care of you, don't you worry."

* * * *

"Alda! Alda, what's wrong? Who is this?" Royce yelled into the phone. He was standing by the bar with his brothers and their friends. They were waiting to hear from Alda for a time to pick her up.

"What is it?" Brew asked with concern. Royce covered his ear with his hand.

"Fuck," he heard someone yell and then Haley's name and then Tatum's.

"Something is wrong," he yelled and ordered them to come with him. Their friends followed and they headed outside as he explained what he heard and the phone went dead.

"Her office, now," he yelled and they rushed to get there.

"What do you think they did? You think they took her?" Logic asked.

"It sounds like it from what you said," Lenox added. Ziek, Jack, and Harley were in the SUV behind them. They hurried to Alda's office building.

By the time they got there she was gone. Haley was nowhere to be found and hardly anyone was in the office.

"Where the hell could they have taken her? Do you know where they live or are staying?" Harley asked them.

"Look who I found," Brew stated, dragging Haley by her hair down the hallway.

"I told you all I know. I'll call the police."

"And tell them what? You helped abduct our woman? I heard you on the phone, bitch. Now tell us where the two dicks took her," Royce yelled at her.

"I don't know anything," she said. Brew shoved her up against the wall and pulled out his gun. He placed it under her chin.

"Do you know who we are? What our profession is?" She shook her head.

"Let's just say if someone needs to get rid of someone and doesn't want to get caught, we eliminate them for fun," he said with clenched teeth. Tears filled her eyes.

"Holy shit," she whispered.

"Talk," Harley ordered.

* * * *

"What's going on? Why did all those men run out of here?" C.J. asked one of the security guys that worked for the Coglonie men.

"Something happened to their girlfriend Alda. They're fucking pissed."

"Alda? What happened?" C.J. asked and tried to push past him to find out from Dominick and the guys.

The guard grabbed him by his shirt. "Whoa, it isn't your concern."

"The hell it isn't. Alda is my cousin."

The guard's eyes widened.

"Come on," he said and pulled C.J. along with him to Dominick and Angelo.

"What is going on with Alda? I heard something about her being hurt," he asked Dominick.

"We don't know yet. Her boyfriend Royce got a call from her. She must have hit the phone and dialed without anyone knowing and it seems two guys doing business at her company may be after her."

"Oh God, they hurt her?" he asked.

"We don't know, C.J. It sounded like maybe they gave her something. She was out of it, saying she didn't feel well and asked for help," Angelo stated.

C.J. ran his fingers through his hair. "Oh God, the drug. They gave her the pill. Shit," he said and paced then went to take out his phone. Dominick grabbed it from him and the guard grabbed C.J.

"Wait, what do you know about this?" Angelo demanded to know.

"I don't know much. Just that if it's the two guys she works with, the one in the picture from the newspaper article, then he's a bad dude."

"What do you mean, a bad dude and what about the drugs you're talking about?"

C.J. panicked, Fogerty was going to kill him but his cousin was more important.

"I could get killed," he said.

Dominick grabbed him by his shirt and gave him a shake.

"Do you know Royce, Brew, Train, and Logic?" He nodded. "Then you'd better tell us everything you know right now, or you'll wish all someone did was put a bullet in your head. Those men torture before they kill, and who knows what they'd do to someone who got their girlfriend hurt, or worse. Now talk."

* * * *

"It all makes sense, but we still don't know where they took Alda, Dominick," Train said into the phone. He had it on speaker. They were all there with their friends trying to find her. They checked the penthouse where the two men lived, the airport to see if they flew somewhere, and nothing.

"I'm getting Garlitto in on this. He's fucking pissed that these dicks were using his territory behind his back, and that Lou Carvetti and Salento Sorenno were working with these men to bring this drug into our clubs and streets. He's putting an end to it. He'll find out where they took her. Hang tight and I'll call you as soon as I hear from him."

"Okay," Train said and ended the call.

"Can you believe this shit? These fucking nobodies come in here and try to do this under our noses and sell this crap?" Harley said.

"I never liked that fucking Carvetti and nor did Collin and Fedarro. I know he did some small things for Dominick and them but still, the guy wanted to be big fast," Jack said to them.

"I would love to put a beating on these dicks for what they did to Alessa, getting that shit out there. I don't even want to think about how those men could have hurt her at the party they planned on taking her to," Lenox said.

"It sounds like they gave that shit to Alda. We need to find her fast," Logic said, reminding them of the severity of the drug and how incapacitated it would make her and susceptible to the two men.

Royce slammed his hand down on the steering wheel. "Come on and call already. Fuck, if they touch her, hell, rape her—"

"Don't, Royce. We'll get them. It's a good thing her cousin was in the club tonight. It saved us time running in circles and also helps to stop this fucked up drug from circulating into the clubs and city."

The phone rang and it was Dominick.

"They took her to a house in the country. Forty minutes north from the G.W. Guys, there's something else we found out. It seems that Tatum, Antonio's cousin, gives the drugs to women a lot but apparently killed a woman."

"What?" Brew asked.

"We found out from Garlitto as his guys interrogated C.J.'s friend Fogerty."

"That dick that hit on Alda and Alessa that night at the club," Lenox stated.

"What did Fogerty say?" Train asked.

"That a few guys were called in for cleanup. That Tatum went crazy and beat the hell out of the woman and killed her. He was on something."

"Let's move. Time is running out quickly," Logic said and they ended the call and headed to the address.

"Forty fucking minutes. Jesus, we aren't going to get to her in time," Brew stated.

"We will. We'll get to her and those men will wish they never touched your woman or tried to push into our territory," Cobra stated.

* * * *

"Look at her, Antonio. She wants it. She does want us," Tatum said and smiled. Alda was pressing her arms above her head and moving around on the bed. He climbed up and stretched over her, cupping her cheek and then her breast.

"So beautiful and giving. You like this bed, Alda?" Tatum asked.

"Mmm, it's soft, and I'm so tired," she said in a seductive moan.

He lowered down and kissed her. She put her arms around his shoulders and he pressed between her thighs.

"That's right, baby. You are going to be spending a lot of time in this bed. By the time we're done with you, you'll know who you belong to," he said to her.

"Brew," she whispered.

Antonio stopped where he was. Tatum lifted up and gripped her arms.

"What did you say?" he asked.

"She's high, Tatum. She doesn't know what's going on and that's what we want. We'll keep her drugged. Get her used to our touch.

Months from now, she'll be under complete control." Antonio stroked her jaw and then down her chest.

"Train," she whispered when Antonio cupped her breast.

"It's Tatum and Antonio. Say it." Tatum raised his voice.

"Tatum." She moaned and moved to the side. Antonio pulled her on top of him and kissed her mouth, her neck.

"That's right, baby. Holy shit, you have one hell of a body on you," Antonio said as Tatum unzipped her dress.

"A fucking tattoo. She has a tattoo," Tatum stated, feeling aroused and ready to take her.

He pulled off his shirt and Antonio rolled her to her back and began to undress her. Her breasts swayed in the very sheer, sexy bra she wore and as they pulled down her dress, they saw the tiny thong panties, the tattoo and belly ring.

"I told you. I fucking told you she was perfect," Tatum said and then began to touch her, caress her skin and then lick along the tattoo.

"Train, please. Oh. Train." She moaned and gripped Antonio's shoulder and Tatum's hair.

"Fuck." Tatum gripped her hips and shook her. "Tatum. The name is Tatum. Say it," he demanded and she moaned and shook her head.

"Train."

He struck her across the mouth. Antonio grabbed his arm.

"No, Tatum, she doesn't know what she's saying. She's high, remember?"

"No. She can say our names. Make her say our names."

Tatum pulled her up and she grabbed at him. He dropped her back down.

"Grab her arms and hold her."

"Oh, Royce. Royce, please," she yelled and lifted her hips.

"Fuck," Tatum yelled and gripped her face hard. "Tatum. Say Tatum," he yelled at her. She wiggled her legs and kicked them. He struck her again.

"Just do it already. She'll learn, Tatum. We don't want her beaten and ugly. Look at what you did to her face, her lips and eye. What the fuck, Tatum."

"Fuck you, she's mine and I'll do with her what I like and what I want. I can't listen to her say their names. She should be saying ours."

Tatum started to undo his pants. Her mouth was bleeding, her cheek swollen when suddenly the lights in the bedroom went out.

"What the fuck?" Tatum said.

Antonio released her arms. "Something is wrong."

"Nothing is wrong. I'm going to take her. You can fuck around with the power." He gripped her hips and the sound of footsteps coming up the stairs like an army of people and then the door burst open. He had his pants down and felt the hit to his head.

* * * *

Brew took out Tatum and Train took out Antonio. Logic and Royce hurried to the bed. The sight of Alda, lying in only her panties and bra, dress ripped from her body, face battered and bleeding, made Royce wince. She was moaning and completely out of it.

"Alda, baby, come on," Logic said her name and caressed her arm.

"Get her out of here. We'll take out the trash," Cobra said to Royce and Logic.

"We'll help and meet you at the penthouse," Brew said straight-faced. They nearly got to her too late. The sight of Tatum standing between her legs with his pants down ready to rape their woman would haunt his thoughts forever.

He felt the hand on his shoulder as Royce held her in his arms and carried her from the room. "You got to her in time. That's what matters," Turbo told him and Logic as they quickly went through the house and out to the SUV.

"Bastards. We should have made them suffer," Logic stated, wiping the blood from her lips as she moaned and held on to Royce.

"It's over. Two less scumbags walk this earth hurting innocent women. Protecting Alda is our number one priority," Royce said and they headed home.

Epilogue

"Whose house is this?" Alda asked as the SUV pulled into the driveway of a really nice house in the suburban neighborhood in New Jersey. It had been a few weeks since the incident at work. Surprisingly she remembered the meeting and the funny feeling she had after drinking the water. From there on out was blank, and what she insisted on her men telling her made her love them even more.

They spent so much time together and she declined being the cover model for MAX Industries cosmetics line but remained on board at Maxwell's insistence as CEO of the company. She would be working with Max hand in hand, hiring on new staff and working to maintain their reputation here in the US for the time being. Haley was fired by Maxwell and threatened by multiple organized crime families, including her men. The drug situation was destroyed, as only Antonio and Tatum knew how to get the drug or create it. No one knew but anyone involved with the selling and distribution was dealt with by the Garlitto family. She was grateful that Dominick and Royce saved her cousin C.J. from getting killed or beaten for his involvement, considering he helped end it all and save her life. That meant a lot to Dominick and the others, who hired him on to be trained accordingly and by Brew and Train personally.

"It's a surprise, baby. Someone very important to us, and that we wanted you to meet," Royce told her.

When they got to the front door of the beautiful, small home, someone answered the door, a young woman in her thirties and she smiled wide.

"Good afternoon, sirs. She's been waiting very impatiently for all of you to arrive."

"Thank you, Liza. This is Alda," he said to her and the woman smiled.

"Nice to meet you, ma'am." She nodded.

"She a caretaker for our—"

"Oh my goodness. She's gorgeous!" the older woman stated as she stood by the hallway looking old, yet strong and spirited.

"Mom," Logic said, surprising Alda. She heard all about Abigail James and how she was their foster mother and helped to save them from the streets of New York. In the past few weeks they explained about their good times and bad. Brew's stint in jail for assault as he helped protect a young woman, and their crimes they got away with, but then their education and achievements all because of one another and Abigail.

"Come here, Alda," Logic said after the men greeted their mom.

"Mom, meet Alda Ruffinno. The woman we're all in love with," Train said, shocking Alda by his confession of love and making tears hit her eyes. The older woman opened her arms to Alda and she hugged her, inhaling that lavender scent Brew secretly told her about and how comforting it had been as a child who was neglected and scared.

She pulled back and Brew pulled her close and kissed her neck.

"Let's enjoy some lunch outside. I want to hear all about how you found Alda and finally let down your guards and fell in love. I have the feeling it's going to be one hell of a love story with you four troublemakers," their mom said and she laughed. They moaned and groaned.

"Troublemakers? We were your favorites," Royce said to her, helping their mom down the two stairs and to the screened in porch. There was another woman setting up lunch and pouring iced tea. It seemed the four men got their mom people to take care of her and provide for her. They were giving back, or at least trying to give her what she provided for them years ago.

"So Alda doesn't know about your pasts," their mom teased.

"She knows some of it, Mom, and still wants us. So don't go messing it all up and scaring her," Train said to their mom as they all gathered around the porch.

"Oh, Alda doesn't look like she'll get scared off. She looks strong, and loves each of you, I can tell. Don't know why you waited to tell her until today," their mom said.

Alda laughed aloud. Brew squeezed her hand.

"You know us, mom."

"Yes, I do. Stubborn, hard-headed men but men I'm proud of." She smiled.

"Now, stories about their childhood. Where to begin," their mom teased and rubbed her hands together like Train did so often. It made her think about their relationship with this woman, how they were orphans and learned to accept her love and even pick up on her expressions and personality. They were opening up to Alda more and more each day, and she knew today was a big deal. Them bringing her to meet their mom and to learn about their troubled childhoods and the miracle they received when Abigail took them in. No wonder they called themselves brothers. They truly were, and she was now part of this family.

When it was time to say good-bye Abigail asked when they would visit again and the men made plans to come next week with Alda but to take their mom out to dinner. By the time they got to the SUV and were driving back to the city, Alda felt so content and loved by them. She didn't think she could be any happier than she was right now.

"What did you think of Mom?" Royce asked her.

"She's so nice, such a big heart and caring woman. I think it's awesome that you all take care of her and have people here to help her so she doesn't have to lift a finger unless she wants to. It's very sweet," she told them.

Brew lifted her up onto his lap and she held on to his shoulders. "Don't tell anyone though. We need to keep our bad ass reps," he said and winked. She cupped his cheek.

"Oh, I know all too well about the reputations you need to keep, Mr. Bad Ass," she said and they chuckled.

"Someone is still needing some training, I see," Royce said.

"I think it's going to take many, many days and nights of your training."

"Are you sure you can accept us the way we are, Alda? Not mushy and all sappy and shit," Train asked and she smiled, glancing over toward him as she sat on Brew's lap.

"Oh, I accept all of you just the way you are. I've loved you for a while now. I didn't want to scare you and tell you. Something like that could send Brew over the edge," she teased,

"What? Why wouldn't you tell us? We said no secrets."

"Well, you kept this secret from me, and waited until you were in front of your mom to tell me you all loved me."

"Mom asked us if we told you yet and we said no, so she asked that we tell you when she was present so she got to at least hear it first as a memory of what she's wished for us for some time," Royce confessed.

"Awe…that is so, so sweet. Totally not bad ass, Brew, sorry," she said.

"Why, you little stinker." Brew dipped her over Train's seat and both men tickled her. She laughed and screamed for them to stop but then those tickles turned to caresses, and more. Train kissed her lips and Brew stroked her thighs, pushed up her skirt and dipped fingers into her cunt. These men were full throttle sexy, dominant men and she loved them with all her heart. Even if their ways of communication were totally non-traditional. Either way, they left her needy for their touch, desperate for their love because with these four men it was all or nothing, and she was just fine with that because they loved her and she loved them.

THE END

WWW.DIXIELYNNDWYER.COM

Siren Publishing, Inc.
www.SirenPublishing.com

Lightning Source UK Ltd.
Milton Keynes UK
UKHW02f1916201117
313065UK00008B/182/P